'TDH doctor, serious and deep—with principles—seeks bright, sparkly female to make his dimples come out. Looking for foodie film buff who enjoys seaside strolls for friendship leading to potential romance.'

He groaned again. 'I hate that bit about the dimples. It sounds really pathetic.'

'Tough. It's staying. Your dimples are cute.' She flicked back to her list. 'You know, Ellis, this list could be describing *you*.'

His heart skipped a beat.

Was this the chance he'd been looking for? Was she telling him in her quiet, understated way that she'd consider dating him?

'And my list,' he said softly, 'could be describing *you*.'

They looked at each other, and it felt as if the air was humming.

'Maybe,' he said, 'neither of us needs to put an ad on the dating site.'

She didn't pull away or look horrified at the idea.

So he leaned forward and gave in to what he'd wanted to do for a year or more. He touched his mouth very lightly to hers.

Dear Reader,

I've always liked friends-to-lovers stories, but this one has a slight twist in that the hero is also the best friend of the heroine's late husband.

And when friendship turns to love when do you dare to take the risk of wrecking the friendship?

A Promise...to a Proposal? is about how Ruby and Ellis take that particular journey—from Ellis promising his best friend that he'll look after his widow to both of them falling in love.

The story's set partly in my bit of the world (or a fictionalised bit of the East Anglian coast), partly in London, and partly in a very beautiful city that I had the privilege to explore earlier this year—Prague. (And I'm afraid I stole the posh dinner my family and I had—the best meal we've ever eaten!)

I hope you enjoy Ellis and Ruby's story.

I'm always delighted to hear from readers, so do come and visit me at katehardy.com

With love

Kate Hardy

A PROMISE...
TO A PROPOSAL?

BY
KATE HARDY

This· and
inci· ·eal
life· ·s
esta· ·e is
enti

This· vay of
trad· lated
with· ng or
cov· nilar
con· quent
pur·

® a· wner
and· with the

United Kingdom Patent Office and/or the Office for Harmonisation in
the Internal Market and in other countries.

First published in Great Britain 2015
by Mills & Boon, an imprint of Harlequin (UK) Limited,
Eton House, 18-24 Paradise Road, Richmond, Surrey, TW9 1SR

© 2015 Pamela Brooks

ISBN: 978-0-263-25844-8

Harlequin (UK) Limited's policy is to use papers that are natural,
renewable and recyclable products and made from wood grown in
sustainable forests. The logging and manufacturing processes conform
to the legal environmental regulations of the country of origin.

Printed and bound in Great Britain
by CPI Antony Rowe, Chippenham, Wiltshire

Kate Hardy lives in Norwich, in the east of England, with her husband, two young children, one bouncy spaniel and too many books to count! When she's not busy writing romance or researching local history she helps out at her children's schools. She also loves cooking—spot the recipes sneaked into her books! (They're also on her website, along with extracts and the stories behind her books.)

Writing for Mills & Boon® has been a dream come true for Kate—something she wanted to do ever since she was twelve. She's been writing Medical Romance™ for over ten years now. She says it's the best of both worlds, because she gets to learn lots of new things when she's researching the background to a book: add a touch of passion, drama and danger, a new gorgeous hero every time, and it's the perfect job!

Kate's always delighted to hear from readers, so do drop in to her website at katehardy.com

Books by Kate Hardy

Mills & Boon® Medical Romance™

Mills & Boon® Cherish™

Visit the author profile page at millsandboon.co.uk for more titles

To Gerard, Chris and Chloe—
remembering the best meal we've ever eaten!

CHAPTER ONE

'HERE?' RUBY ASKED.

'It's a sandy beach, we're below the high tide line, the tide's coming in right now and the wind's in the right direction—so I'd say it's just about perfect,' Ellis said.

Well, it would've been perfect if it hadn't been drizzling with rain. But today was what it was, and the weather didn't matter. Just as it hadn't mattered a year ago. The day that had blown a hole in all their lives.

She smiled. 'Tom always did say you were the practical one.'

And the one with itchy feet who could never stay in one place for long.

Except for the last eighteen months, which Ellis had spent in London solely because of Tom, his best friend since their first day at infant school. They'd gone to university together, and trained together in the same London hospital. When Tom had been diagnosed with leukaemia, that had been the one thing to bring Ellis back to England. He'd wanted to be there for his best friend and support him through to the end. Ellis had promised Tom in those last agonising months that he'd be there for Ruby, too, and support her through at least the first year after Tom's death.

Including today.

Which was why he was walking on the beach on a drizzly September day with Tom's parents and Ruby, on the first anniversary of Tom's death, to help them scatter some of Tom's ashes in his favourite place. A place that brought back so many happy childhood memories that it put a lump in Ellis's throat.

'Thanks for looking up all the information for us,' Ruby said. 'I wasn't sure if we had to get permission from someone first or even how you go about scattering ashes.'

'Hey, it's the least I could do. I loved Tom, too,' Ellis said. And when Ruby had first broached the subject about scattering Tom's ashes, he'd known exactly where Tom would've wanted it to be.

He spread a couple of waterproof blankets on the beach for the four of them to kneel on, and took four brightly coloured spades and buckets from a plastic bag.

It might be a dark day, the final goodbye, but Ellis wanted to remember the brightness. To remember Tom as he was before he was ill and to celebrate the close friendship they'd shared over the years.

'I remember you boys doing this when you were small,' Brenda said with a wobble in her voice as she dug into the sand and filled her bucket. 'You both loved the beach. It didn't matter if it was summer or winter— if we asked you what you wanted to do, you'd both beg to come here and make sandcastles.'

The lump in Ellis's throat meant he couldn't speak. He remembered. Days when life was simple. Days when his parents had been as carefree as Tom's. Though Tom's parents, he knew, wouldn't react in the same way as his parents had when it came to the death of their child. Brenda and Mike would talk about Tom with love and keep him alive in their hearts, rather than stonewalling everything.

Working in companionable silence, the four of them made a sandcastle. Just as they had when Tom and Ellis were small boys: only this time Tom's widow was taking Tom's place.

When they'd finished, Ellis produced a flag from his bag—one made from an ice-lolly stick and a photograph of Tom. It was one of his favourite memories: the day they'd opened their A level results together, whooped, and known they were both going to train as doctors in London. For Tom, it had been the next step towards a dream. For Ellis, it had been the next step towards escape from a home that had come to feel like a mausoleum.

'He was eighteen years old then,' Mike said softly as Ellis handed him the flag. 'With the whole world before him.'

How very little time Tom had actually had. Not even half a lifetime.

And how very much Ellis wished his best friend was still here. 'He was special,' Ellis said, his voice cracking.

'Yes. He was,' Mike said, and put the flag on the top turret.

Brenda and Ruby both gulped hard and squeezed each other's hand.

Ellis finished digging the moat round the outside of the castle; and then the four of them took turns scattering Tom's ashes in the moat and covering them over with sand. Ruby sprinkled rose petals on the top.

Then Ellis moved the blankets back a little way, set

up the two huge umbrellas he'd packed in the car when he'd seen the weather report, and uncorked a bottle of champagne.

'To Tom,' he said when he'd filled their glasses. 'And may our memories of him make the smiles outnumber the tears.' Even though right now it felt as if the tears were more than outweighing the smiles, Ellis was determined to celebrate his friend rather than be selfish about his loss.

Mike, Brenda and Ruby echoed the toast, even though their smiles were wobbly and Ellis could see their eyes were shiny with tears they tried to blink away.

Then the four of them sat and watched as the tide came in, slowly sweeping the sandcastle away with the ashes, and tumbling the rose petals and Tom's photograph in the waves.

Afterwards, Ellis drove Tom's parents home.

'Will you come in for something to eat?' Brenda asked on the doorstep.

'Thanks, but...' Ellis tailed off. Even being in this town made him feel stifled. He hated it here. What he really wanted to do was drive as fast as he could back to London. Away from the dark memories.

'Of course. You'll want to drop in to see your own mum while you're here,' Brenda said.

Ellis didn't have the heart to disillusion her, so he just smiled. Today of all days, he really couldn't face his parents. They'd be aware of what he'd just been doing, and they'd be thinking of Sally. And, as always, they'd retreat into coolness rather than talk to him or even give him a sympathetic hug. Even though Ellis understood why—when you'd lost someone you loved so very much, sometimes withdrawing from everyone seemed like the only way to keep your heart safe from further hurt—he still found it hard to deal with. He always felt as if he'd lost more than his beloved only sister, twenty years ago; he'd lost his parents, too. And although he'd remained reasonably close to his older brothers, his choice of career had put a distinct rift between them. Tom's parents had been Ellis's greatest support through his teen years, and he'd always be grateful to them for it. And for Tom's sake he'd look out for them now, the way they'd looked out for him.

Brenda hugged him. 'Thank you for being there for us.'

'Any time.' And he meant it. 'Just because Tom's...' He couldn't say the word. He just *couldn't*. 'Not here,' he said croakily, 'it doesn't mean you're not still part of my life, because you are. You know I think of you as my second set of parents. I always will.'

Tears glittered in Brenda's eyes. She patted his shoulder, clearly too moved to talk, and then hugged Ruby.

'I'll text you when we get back to London,' Ruby promised.

But she looked quizzically at Ellis when he drove straight out of the town and back towards London. 'I thought you were going to see your parents?'

'Not today.'

'Look, don't feel you have to get me back to London if you want to see them. I can always go back to Brenda and Mike's and wait until you're ready, or get the train back.'

That was the point. He didn't actually want to see his parents. Especially not today. Part of him lambasted himself for being selfish, but the realistic part of him knew it was necessary self-preservation. 'Another time,' he said.

'If you're sure.'

'Oh, I'm sure,' he said softly. 'My parents are... complicated.'

She reached over and squeezed his hand briefly. 'I know,' she said, equally softly.

In the months since Tom's death, Ellis had opened up a little to Ruby and told her about the tragedy that had taken the sunshine out of his world. How his older sister had taken a gap year before university, teaching in a remote school. Sally had fallen pregnant by accident and hadn't realised it at first; when she'd been so sick, everyone had assumed it was a virus. But by the time they'd realised she was suffering from hyperemesis gravidarum, a severe form of morning sickness, it was too late. She'd grown too weak, developed complications, gone into organ failure and never regained consciousness.

And Ellis's parents had never recovered from losing their only daughter. Their remaining three sons simply hadn't been enough to bring them back from the cold, emotionless life they'd led from that moment on.

Ellis and Ruby drove back in companionable silence, listening to Nick Drake. The kind of mellow, faintly melancholy stuff Ellis had enjoyed listening to with Tom. It went well with the rain and his mood.

Back in London, he parked in the street outside Ruby's house and saw her to the door.

'Thank you, for today, Ellis. I don't know what I would have done this last year without you,' she said.

'Hey, no problem—and you've helped me, too.' He hugged her. Bad move. Now he could smell her perfume, the sweet scent of violets. And she fitted perfectly in his arms.

She's your best friend's widow, he reminded himself silently. No, no and absolutely no. Don't even *think* about it. You do not make a move on this woman. Ever. Hands off.

'I'll see you at work tomorrow,' he said. 'Call me if you need me.'

'Thanks, Ellis.' She reached up and kissed his cheek.

For a moment, Ellis desperately wanted to twist his face to the side so the kiss landed on his mouth. For months now he'd wanted to kiss Ruby. But he held himself back. The feelings he'd developed towards her over the last year were completely inappropriate; plus he risked losing one of his closest friendships if he asked her out. He was pretty sure that Ruby saw him only as a friend, so wanting more was just *stupid*. Especially as he knew he wasn't a good bet when it came to relationships.

His normal job, working for a medical aid charity, meant that relationships were tricky. Either he had long-distance affairs where he hardly ever saw his girlfriend and the relationship ended by mutual agreement because his girlfriend just got fed up waiting for him; or they were short, sweet flings that ended when he moved on to another assignment. Except for his marriage to Natalia—he'd thought that would be the exception to the rule, that maybe he could have the best of both worlds after all. How wrong he'd been there. So nowadays he didn't do more than short, fun flings—where everyone knew the score before they started and nobody ended up disappointed.

When Ruby was finally ready to move on, Ellis knew

she'd want more than just a fling or a long-distance relationship. More than he could offer her. Asking for more than friendship would just ruin a relationship that had become really important to him over the last eighteen months. And to have her solely as his friend was way better than not having her in his life at all, wasn't it? So he'd just have to keep himself in check.

'I'd better go,' he mumbled, and left before he did something really reckless and stupid. Like kissing her.

And he brooded all the way home. His current job as an obstetrician at the London Victoria was only temporary, covering another registrar's maternity leave, and his contract was due to end in a couple of months' time when Billie was due to return. He'd already agreed to do a month's assignment for the medical aid charity, helping to set up a new medical centre in Zimbabwe, when his temporary contract at the London Victoria ended. Going to work abroad again would mean he'd be out of temptation's way and he wouldn't hurt Ruby.

Then again, Ellis had promised Tom that he'd look after Ruby. Until he knew that she was ready to move on and had found someone else to share her life—someone who was good enough for her and would treat her as she deserved—how could he desert her?

It was a tricky line to walk.

So he'd just have to bury his feelings, the way he normally did, and everything would be just fine.

Ruby watched Ellis drive away, feeling guilty. For a moment she'd been tempted to kiss him on the lips instead of on the cheek.

How could she possibly want to kiss another man? And especially how could she have thoughts like that on the first anniversary of her husband's death? How mean-spirited and selfish and plain *wrong* was that?

She closed the door with a grimace of self-disgust.

Plus she knew that Tom had asked Ellis to look out for her. Letting Ellis know that she was starting to see him as more than a friend might make everything go wrong between them. He'd always been such a perfect gentleman towards her. Trying to push their friendship in another direction might mean that she lost him—and she didn't want that to happen. She liked having Ellis in her life. Liked it a lot.

Though she had a nasty feeling that she was going to lose him anyway. Ellis had always had itchy feet, according to Tom, and she knew that Ellis wanted to go back to the medical aid charity. The place where he'd always felt he'd belonged.

Losing Tom had ripped Ruby's heart to shreds. Over the last year, she'd gradually put the pieces back together, and it would be very stupid to let herself fall for someone who'd made it very clear that he didn't do permanent. Someone who didn't want the same things she wanted. Someone she knew she'd lose to his job. Yes, he would come back to England from time to time to see her—but she'd be lonely in London, waiting for him. Yet, if she went with him, she'd end up feeling horribly homesick and missing her family. Neither option was right for her. Which meant that Ellis really wasn't the right man for her, much as she was attracted to him, and she needed to think with her head rather than her heart.

Now they'd scattered Tom's ashes and she was back in London again, Ruby didn't quite know what to do with herself. She wished she'd asked Ellis to go somewhere for dinner with her or something; right now, she felt so *lonely*.

She mooched around for the best part of an hour, not able to settle to reading or doing crosswords. Even cleaning the bathroom until it sparkled didn't make her feel as if she'd achieved anything; she was in limbo.

Then the doorbell rang.

Her heart leapt. Had Ellis come back?

No, of course not. How stupid of her to think it.

She opened the door to see her best friend, Tina, bearing what looked suspiciously like a box of home-made cake.

'With today being what it is, I thought you could do with some company tonight,' Tina said, 'and this.' She lifted the box. 'Lemon cake.'

Ruby's favourite. And Ruby knew without a doubt Tina had made it especially for her. It was probably still warm.

'There isn't anyone in the world I'd rather see right now,' Ruby said, meaning it. Not even Ellis. Because with her best friend Ruby knew she wouldn't have that edge of guilt and faint shame that she seemed to feel around Ellis nowadays, outside work. 'Thank you. Thank you so much.' She hugged her best friend, hard.

Tina hung her coat in the hallway and made herself at home in the kitchen, putting the kettle on and getting the teapot out of the cupboard, the way she and Ruby had done hundreds of times over the years in each other's kitchens. 'So how did it go this afternoon?'

'Really well. It didn't matter that it was raining. Ellis had brought a couple of huge umbrellas and waterproof blankets for us to sit on.' Ruby smiled. 'We made a sandcastle and put the ashes in the moat, covered it with rose petals, toasted Tom with champagne and let the sea wash the sandcastle and the ashes away together.'

'It sounds perfect—well, as perfect as something like that could be.' Tina finished making the tea, put the lemon cake on the plate and cut them both a slice, then handed Ruby a steaming mug. 'To Tom,' she said, lifting her mug and clinking it against Ruby's. 'I'll miss him horribly. But I'll always be glad I knew him, because he was just the nicest guy in the world.'

'Yeah.' Ruby took a sip of her tea to take the lump out of her throat.

'Hey. It's OK to cry,' Tina said softly.

'No. I want to remember him with smiles, not tears,' Ruby insisted. 'He wouldn't have wanted anyone to be miserable.'

'But?'

Ruby and Tina had clicked immediately when they'd met on the first day of their nursing training at the age of eighteen, and they'd been friends for long enough to have a pretty good idea what each other wasn't saying.

'I feel a bit guilty, that's all.' Ruby wasn't quite ready to admit her feelings for Ellis, but she also knew that Tina was the best person she could float ideas past. Someone who'd be honest with her.

'Why on earth do you feel guilty?' Tina looked puzzled.

'Because tomorrow it'll be a year and a day—the last traditional day of mourning—and over those last months Tom said to me quite a few times that he didn't want me to be alone and grieving for him. He said he wanted me to live a happy life with someone who loves me as much as he did.'

'Now you're putting a lump in my throat.' Tina

hugged her. 'Though he's right—you're still young. In fact, at twenty-nine you're practically a baby.'

Ruby laughed. There were all of six months between them, with Ruby being one of the youngest in their academic year and Tina one of the oldest. 'Thirty's not exactly old, Tina.'

'No.' Tina looked at her. 'Rubes, are you saying you want to date again?'

'I love Tom—I always will—but I think I'm ready to move on. Scattering his ashes today felt a lot like closure,' Ruby said. 'But is everyone going to think I'm heartless and I should wait a lot longer before even thinking about moving on?'

'No. Some people will probably mutter about it being too soon,' Tina said, 'but remember that you can't please all of the people all of the time, so don't let that get to you. It's none of their business. You're the only one who can really say when you're ready.'

'I guess.' Ruby bit her lip. 'I just...' She shook her head and sighed. 'Sorry.'

'As you said, Tom wanted you to be happy and he wanted you to find someone else. You have his blessing, and you don't need anyone else's.'

Even if I fell for his best friend?

But Ruby couldn't quite bring herself to ask that. She'd barely admitted it to herself and she still needed time to get used to the idea.

'You know, we've got a new registrar in Neurology. He's a nice guy. Single. New to London. Maybe...' Tina let the suggestion hang in the air.

'Maybe,' Ruby said.

'Don't make a decision now. Just think about it,' Tina

said gently. 'In the meantime, I think we need a feel-good film and more cake.'

'Brilliant idea. Let's do it,' Ruby said, and ushered her best friend into the living room.

But she found it hard to concentrate on the film, because she couldn't stop thinking about Ellis. Ellis, with his haunted grey eyes. Ellis, who had itchy feet but had stayed in one place for the longest time since his training, specifically to be there for her.

Her husband's best friend.

What if...?

CHAPTER TWO

RUBY EXAMINED MRS HARRIS GENTLY.

'So is everything OK?' Mrs Harris asked anxiously.

'I'm happy with how you're doing,' Ruby said, 'but we do have a tiny complication, in that your little one is quite happy being bottom-down rather than top-down. So I just want a quick chat with the doctor to talk through your options for the birth.'

Mrs Harris bit her lip. 'So the baby's in the wrong position?'

'Bottom-first rather than head-first—it's called being a breech baby,' Ruby explained. 'It's a really common position in early pregnancy, but the baby usually turns by itself into the head-first position before birth. Your baby hasn't turned yet, that's all.'

'Does it mean there's something wrong with the baby?' Mrs Harris asked.

'No. It happens with about three in a hundred babies, and there are all kinds of reasons for it, some of them being plain baby awkwardness because they want to do things their way rather than follow their mum's birth plan,' Ruby reassured her. 'I'll just go and get Dr Webster, and then we can talk it through with him.' She squeezed Mrs Harris's hand. 'Try not to worry. There

are a few things we can do to persuade the baby to turn.'
She smiled, and went to find Ellis in his office.

Her heart skipped a beat when she saw him. Ellis
was wearing a charcoal grey suit, a white shirt and an
understated tie rather than green Theatre scrubs, and he
looked utterly gorgeous. He wouldn't have looked out
of place on the pages of a glossy magazine as a model
for an upmarket perfume house.

And she needed to stop herself thinking like this.
Ellis was her friend and her colleague. Asking for more
was just greedy.

She tapped on the open door and leaned against the
jamb. 'Hey, Ellis. Can I borrow you for a second?'

He looked up and smiled at her, and her heart skipped
another beat.

'Sure. Problem?' he asked.

'Complication,' she said. 'I have a first-time mum
who's thirty-seven weeks. Her baby's quite happily settled in the breech position. I know her birth plan is
firmly centred round a natural birth with no intervention.' And she also knew that a lot of doctors would
take one look at Mrs Harris's situation and immediately
insist on a caesarean section. Given Ellis's experience
outside the hospital, Ruby really hoped that he'd take
a different tack and give Mrs Harris a chance to have
the birth she really wanted. 'So I wondered if you'd
mind coming and chatting through her options for the
birth,' she finished.

'Of course I will. You did warn her that babies never
respect their mum's birth plans, didn't you?'

She smiled back. 'I always do.'

'So what are you thinking?'

'We'll start with an ECV to see if we can get the baby

to turn,' Ruby said. 'But, if it doesn't work, I'm hoping that I can talk one of the obstetricians—' she gave him a pointed look so he'd know she meant him '—into agreeing to a trial of labour for a vaginal breech delivery.'

'I think we've only had a couple on the ward since I've been here, and I wasn't on duty at the time,' Ellis said. 'Are the doctors here not supportive of vaginal breech births?'

'Theo's wonderful,' Ruby said. Theo Petrakis, the director of the maternity ward at the London Victoria, believed in supporting his midwives and keeping intervention to a minimum. 'But, as you say, it's not that common—and I need someone who's had a reasonable amount of experience in delivering breech babies.'

'Which is why you're talking to me?'

She gave him her sweetest smile. 'Got it in one.'

'She's a first-time mum, so we have no guarantee that her pelvis is big enough to cope.' Ellis looked thoughtful. 'OK. If ECV doesn't work then—on condition the baby's not too big or small, the baby's head isn't tilted back and I'm happy that the mum's pelvis is going to cope—I'll support you and you can call me in, even if I'm not on duty when she goes into labour. But in return I need a favour from you.'

Ruby's heart skipped yet another beat. What was he going to ask for?

A kiss?

She shook herself mentally. How ridiculous. She really had to stop fantasising about Ellis. This was totally inappropriate. They were at work, and she needed to keep her professionalism to the forefront. 'Sure. What do you want?'

'I'd like you to talk your mum into letting a couple

of the junior staff observe their first ever breech birth. One midwife, one doctor.'

'Great minds think alike. I was going to ask you if there was anyone you wanted to come and observe.' And she really liked the fact that he'd thought of the midwifery team, too, not just the obstetricians. She smiled. 'I want to reassure Mrs Harris that we'll try our best to help give her the birth experience she really wants, but I'll make it clear that if the baby's in distress at any point then we might need to give her a section, so she needs to be prepared for that to happen.'

'Which is again where I'd come in,' Ellis said.

'Just flutter those disgustingly long eyelashes at her. Actually, on second thoughts, perhaps you'd better not,' she said. 'You already look more like a movie star than a doctor.'

'Very funny, Rubes,' Ellis said, but he didn't look the slightest bit offended.

Which was another reason why she should put this whole thing out of her head. If she made an approach to Ellis and he turned her down…Even though she knew he'd be kind about it, it would still put a strain on their friendship. On their working relationship. And Ruby didn't want to take the risk of wrecking either of them.

Maybe it was just loneliness making her feel this way, and she should take Tina up on her offer of setting her up with the new registrar on the Neurology ward.

'Penny for them?' Ellis asked.

No way was she going to tell Ellis what she was thinking about. 'Just my first-time mum,' she said with a smile. It was true; it just wasn't the *whole* truth.

Back in the examination room, she introduced Ellis. 'Mrs Harris, this is Dr Ellis Webster, one of our registrars. Ellis, this is Mrs Harris. She's a first-time mum, the baby's thirty-seven weeks, and the baby's quite happy in the breech position.'

'Nice to meet you, Mrs Harris.' Ellis shook her hand and smiled at her. 'Ruby tells me that you'd like as natural a birth as possible.'

'I definitely don't want an epidural. I want to manage with gas and air,' Mrs Harris said. 'And I really didn't want to have a section.' She bit her lip. 'But, because the baby's lying the wrong way, does that mean I have to have a section?'

'It's a possibility,' Ellis said, 'but it might be possible for you to have a vaginal delivery. With the baby being breech, it means that the head—which is the biggest part of the baby—is the last bit to be delivered, so it's a little bit more complicated. May I examine you?'

At her nod, he examined her gently.

'As Ruby said, your baby's definitely bottom-down. But we can try to persuade the baby to move. There's a procedure called an ECV, which stands for external cephalic version. Ruby here's very experienced.'

'What happens is that I'll press down on your abdomen and encourage the baby to turn a somersault—a bit like him doing a forward roll inside your stomach,' Ruby explained.

'And it always works?' Mrs Harris asked.

'It works about for about fifty per cent of babies,' Ellis said. 'And if it doesn't work today, then we can always try again tomorrow. Though I should warn you that even if the baby does turn, sometimes the baby then decides to roll back again.'

'So if you do this ECV thing, what about the baby?'

Mrs Harris asked. 'Will he be OK? It's not going to hurt him?'

'He'll be fine,' Ruby reassured her. 'Plus we'll monitor him before, during and after the ECV to keep an eye on him. There is a tiny risk that you might start having contractions, and also the baby's heart rate might go up a bit—usually it settles again pretty quickly, but I do want you to be aware that sometimes the baby's heart rate doesn't settle again, and in that case you'll need to have a section.'

'But it's a tiny risk?' Mrs Harris checked.

'Tiny,' Ruby confirmed.

'All right, then.' Mrs Harris paused. 'Will it hurt me?'

'It can be a bit uncomfortable, yes,' Ruby said. 'But, if it hurts, all you have to do is tell us and we'll stop immediately.'

Mrs Harris looked worried. 'But if it doesn't work, does that mean I'll have to have a section?'

'The baby's a good weight. He's not too big or too small,' Ellis said. 'Though I would want to check that his neck isn't tilted back before I agree to try a vaginal delivery. If the baby's head is tilted back, then I'm afraid you will need a caesarean section, because that'll be the safest thing for the baby.'

'Is there anything else I can do to help the baby turn, or make sure he stays the right way round if you do the ECV? Can I sit or lie in a certain way?' Mrs Harris asked.

Ruby shook her head. 'I'm afraid it won't make any difference.'

'So why hasn't he turned round the right way? Why is he bottom-down instead of head-down?'

'There are lots of reasons,' Ellis said. 'Sometimes

it's down to the position of your placenta. As I said earlier, the biggest part of the baby is the head, so the baby tends to fidget round and make sure he's in the most comfortable position, which means his head will be in the biggest space—in your lower uterus, so he'll be head-down. But if you have a low-lying placenta, then the biggest space is in your upper uterus, so the baby will be bottom-down.' He smiled. 'Sometimes it's just plain old chance. Babies have a habit of doing things their way, and I know a lot of mums who haven't ended up having the birth they'd set their heart on. So all I'd say is please try not to be disappointed if we can't follow your birth plan to the letter.'

'We'll do our best to make it work for you,' Ruby said, 'but Dr Webster's right—at the end of the day, babies can be very stubborn and they'll do things their way.'

'I think this one's going to be like his dad,' Mrs Harris said ruefully. 'Can Ian be here when you try and make the baby turn round?'

'Of course,' Ruby reassured her. 'We can try this afternoon, just after lunch. Will that give him enough time to get here?'

Mrs Harris nodded. 'I'll call him. Thank you. Both of you.'

'I'll see you later this afternoon, Mrs Harris,' Ellis said with a smile.

The rest of Ruby's clinic ran on time. Just as she broke for lunch, she saw Ellis coming out of the staff kitchen. 'Got time for lunch?' he asked.

'That would be nice,' she said.

They headed down to the canteen, chatting companionably. At the counter, Ellis as usual chose the vegetarian option.

'Any excuse to stuff your face with pasta and garlic bread. You're such a carb junkie,' Ruby teased.

'Protein's important, but I've worked in areas where people are so poor and the cost of raising—' He broke off. 'You're teasing me, aren't you?'

'It's very easy to tease you, Ellis—you're so serious,' she said with a smile. 'Look, I know why you're vegetarian and I admire your principles.'

'But you don't share them,' he finished.

She shook her head. 'I'm sorry, but vegetarian bacon is never going to be as good as the real thing for me.'

He laughed. 'You're such a hedonist. Anyway, Rubes, you can talk about being a carb junkie. I've seen you and Tina with cake. It lasts for about three seconds when you two are around.'

'Busted,' Ruby said with a grin.

'Are you OK about doing the ECV this afternoon?' he asked.

'It's fine,' Ruby said. 'I'd really like to bring Coral, our new trainee midwife, in to observe, if Mrs Harris doesn't mind—and if you don't mind.'

'Of course not. You know I agree with you; it's always a good idea to give students as broad an experience as possible.'

'That's one of the things I like about you—you're so practical and sensible. Thanks,' she said.

Practical and sensible. Not how he'd been when he'd married Natalia, Ellis thought wryly. He'd lost his head and they'd both paid the price.

Though Ruby had said that was *one* of the things she

liked about him. He couldn't help wondering: what else did she like about him?

He shook himself. This really wasn't appropriate. Ruby Fisher was his friend. His best friend's girl—well, widow, but that was a technicality. Time to back off. 'I try to be practical,' he said lightly.

'Ellis, I, um, wanted to run something by you,' she said.

She looked worried, and Ellis frowned. 'What's wrong?'

'Not *wrong,* exactly...but today's a year and a day since Tom died.'

Yeah. He knew. He'd spent the anniversary with her on a Suffolk beach yesterday.

'And a year and a day is supposed to be the traditional length of time for mourning.'

He went cold. Where was she going with this?

'I'm never going to forget Tom,' Ruby said, 'but he always told me that he didn't want me to spend the rest of my life mourning for him, and he wanted me to move on.'

Wait—*what*?

Was she saying that she wanted to date again? That she'd met someone? Who? Where? How? Ellis couldn't quite process this.

'And Tina's going to set me up on a blind date with her new colleague in Neurology,' she finished.

Ruby was really going on a date? With someone else? But—but...

'Ellis? You haven't said anything.' She looked even more worried. 'Do you think it's too soon?'

'I...' He blew out a breath. This was a minefield. If he said the wrong thing now, he'd hurt her—and that was the last thing he wanted to do. 'I think,' he said slowly, 'that you're the best one to judge that. Only you know when you're ready.'

But the idea of seeing her with another man made him feel sick.

It was different when she'd been married to Tom. Ellis would never, ever have done anything to destroy his best friend's marriage. But now Ruby was widowed. And Ellis hated the idea of her going out with someone else.

If she really was ready to date again, maybe he could ask her out himself.

But, if she said no, then how could they go back to their old easy friendship, once they knew they didn't feel the same about each other?

He didn't want to risk losing her.

So he was just going to have to suck it up and deal with it. Even if it felt as if someone had just filleted him.

Typical Ellis. Sensible and measured. *I think you're the best one to judge that.*

Which told Ruby without a doubt that he wasn't interested in her. Otherwise that would've been his cue to suggest that she dated him, wouldn't it?

So it was just as well she hadn't suggested anything to him. It would've put an irreparable strain on their friendship, and she valued him too much to risk losing him.

'I guess you're right,' she said. 'I just didn't want people to think that I was the Merry Widow, not caring about Tom. And I feel guilty about wanting to date again.' She felt even more guilty about the fact that she was attracted to Ellis, particularly as he'd just made it clear it wasn't reciprocated.

'You're always going to love him,' Ellis said. 'But at the end of the day life still goes on. And Tom didn't want you to be lonely. He wanted you to be happy. What anyone else thinks is simply their opinion. They have the right to think whatever they like, but they don't have the right to shove it down your throat. You do what makes you happy, Rubes.'

Yeah.

Though sometimes she wondered if she'd ever find that kind of happiness again. If she was being greedy and expecting too much. Some people didn't even have that kind of happiness once in their lives, so what right did she have to expect to find it twice?

Ellis reached over to squeeze her hand, and her skin tingled all the way up her arm.

'Be happy, Ruby. You've got my full support. And if anyone says otherwise, send them to see me and I'll put them straight.'

He sounded as if he were her big brother.

And she'd just have to learn to see him as a kind of sibling instead of the man she wanted to start dating.

After lunch, Ruby called the Harrises in from the waiting area.

'I was wondering—would you mind if Coral, my trainee midwife, came in and observed the procedure?' she asked.

'No, that's fine, love,' Mrs Harris said. 'I'll do whatever you want if you can get this baby to do that forward roll.'

'I'll do my best. Thank you.' She smiled at Mrs Harris.

'I'm going to check how the baby's doing, first, on the ultrasound. If I'm happy with that, I'll give you some drugs to relax your womb—it won't hurt you or the baby, but it'll mean your baby has a bit more room to do that forward roll.'

'All right. Is that nice doctor going to be here?'

'Dr Webster? Yes. He's just making a quick phone call, and then he'll be right here. And I'll go and collect Coral so I can introduce her to you.' Ruby smiled at her. 'Lie back and bare your tummy for me. Though I'm afraid my gel's a little bit colder than it is in the ultrasound suite.'

'I don't mind,' Mrs Harris said, smiling back.

Once Ruby had established that everything was fine, she moved the screen so that the Harrises could see the baby. 'There he is—looking very comfy right now.'

'Hopefully he won't be stubborn and he'll move,' Mrs Harris said wryly.

'I'll give you those drugs now.' Ruby administered them swiftly. 'Make yourself comfortable, and I'll be right back,' she said.

When she returned, Ellis was already there. Ruby introduced the Harrises to Coral.

'So what we're going to do today is an external cephalic version—ECV, for short. The idea is to move the baby's bottom away from his mum's pelvis,' Ruby explained. 'I've already given Mrs Harris some drugs to help relax her womb, and we've seen the baby on the ultrasound. What I'm going to do now, Mrs Harris, is to push firmly on your abdomen to encourage the baby to do a kind of forward roll. It'll take maybe a minute to a minute and a half. As I said earlier, it might be a little bit uncomfortable but it shouldn't hurt. If it does hurt, I need you to tell me straight away and I'll stop.'

'All right.' Mrs Harris looked nervous, and Ruby noticed that she was holding her husband's hand really tightly.

'You might even see him do a forward roll in your tummy, so keep an eye on my hands,' she said with a smile.

Coral came quietly to the side so she could see and, gently but firmly, Ruby performed the manoeuvre, trying to ease the baby into a transverse position before he moved into the head-down position.

But the baby stubbornly refused to move.

After two minutes, Ruby stopped.

'Is something wrong?' Mr Harris asked anxiously.

'No—just that this baby really doesn't want to move today,' Ruby said.

'The longer the procedure takes, the less likely it is to work,' Ellis explained. 'But try not to worry. We can always try again tomorrow.'

They checked the baby again with the ultrasound. 'He's doing just fine,' Ellis reassured the Harrises. He glanced at the notes. 'Actually, his heart rate is pretty much as it was before Ruby started the ECV, so I'm happy for you to go home now, or you can stay in the waiting room until you're ready.'

'If we try again tomorrow and it still doesn't work, that means I'm going to have to have a section, doesn't it?' Mrs Harris asked.

'Not necessarily,' Ruby reassured her. 'Remember what we said this morning. We can still try for a vaginal delivery if the ECV doesn't work next time. We'll just need a bit of patience.'

'If it helps, I've delivered one or two breech babies in the middle of a field before now,' Ellis added.

'In the middle of a *field*?' Mr Harris looked surprised.

'I worked for a medical aid charity for a few years,' Ellis said. 'So I've delivered babies after natural disasters where there isn't even any running water in the area.'

Mrs Harris bit her lip. 'And here I am, moaning about it all, when I know I'm going to have a comfortable bed and all the medical equipment anyone needs! That's terrible. I feel...' She grimaced. 'Well, guilty, now.'

'You really don't need to. This is all new to you, and it's perfectly natural that you're concerned,' Ellis said. 'Actually, I'd be more concerned if you *weren't* worried.'

'I think she should have a section,' Ian Harris said. 'I looked up breech births on the Internet, and they said it's likely that the baby's head will get trapped or the baby will be brain-damaged.'

'The Internet,' Ellis said gently, 'is full of scary stories. It's the same with magazines—they're going to tell you all about the unusual cases and the dramatic stuff, because it's the drama that sells copies. They won't tell you that most women have a perfectly safe, normal delivery. As Ruby says, you just need a bit of patience with a vaginal breech birth. I believe in being hands off and letting the mum set the pace, and I only intervene if there's a problem.'

'So I won't have to have an episiotomy?' Mrs Harris asked.

'Hopefully not. We'll see how it goes,' Ellis said. 'Though I will say that if your labour isn't progressing after an hour, then I'll recommend a section. In my experience, when labour doesn't progress, it means there's a complication and you need help.'

'All right,' Mrs Harris said.

Ruby could see that Mrs Harris was biting back the tears, and sat down on the bed beside her to hold her other hand. 'We'll do our best for you, I promise,' she said softly. 'We're on your side. All we're saying is that if it doesn't work out quite the way you want it to, then please don't blame yourself. You've given it your best shot and that's more than good enough.'

'OK.' But Mrs Harris still looked close to tears.

Ruby hugged her. 'Hang on in there,' she said. 'It's going to be fine.'

CHAPTER THREE

MRS HARRIS CAME in with her husband the next day for another attempt at the ECV. 'I've been feeling a bit off, all day,' she said. 'I woke up in the middle of the night with a bit of a tummy-ache. Obviously I must've eaten something that didn't agree with me last night.'

Or maybe, Ruby thought, it was something else causing that tummy-ache. She had a funny feeling about this—and her funny feelings were usually right.

'Come and lie down, and I'll examine you before we try the ECV again,' she said.

Mrs Harris had just settled back against the bed when she grimaced. 'Sorry. That was another twinge.'

Ruby examined her gently. 'Has anyone mentioned Braxton-Hicks to you?'

'The practice contractions, you mean?'

'They're the ones,' Ruby said.

'Yes—but I don't think I've had any.' Mrs Harris's eyes widened. 'Hang on—is that what the twinges mean? I'm having a practice contraction?'

'Given that you're three centimetres dilated,' Ruby said, 'then, actually, I think this is the real thing.'

'But I'm only thirty-seven weeks! It's too soon for the

baby to be born.' Mrs Harris bit her lip. 'Do you think it was that ECV thing yesterday that's caused this?'

'Possibly. Or it could be that your baby's just decided that his birthday's going to be today,' Ruby said with a smile. 'Don't worry about him being thirty-seven weeks. Not that many babies are born on their official due date—some are a couple of weeks before, and some are ten days or so late. By this stage your baby's lungs are definitely mature enough to cope with being born.'

'So will I have to have a section?'

'Hopefully not,' Ruby said cheerfully. 'I'm just going to get someone to call Dr Webster for me. And I need to give you a scan to see exactly how the baby's lying.'

'Cold gel again?' Mrs Harris asked ruefully.

'I'm afraid so,' Ruby said.

She came out of the cubicle and asked one of the auxiliary staff to find Ellis for her, then went back to see the Harrises and do the scan. She turned the screen so that the Harrises could see it. 'And here we can see one baby getting ready to be born. His head's tucked forward, just as I'd want it to be, and he's in what we call the frank breech position—that's the least complicated one, with his legs straight up in front of him.'

'So I can try for a normal birth?' Mrs Harris asked.

Ellis arrived in time to hear the question. 'I examined you yesterday and I'm happy that your pelvis is big enough to cope with having the baby. He's not too small, so there's a lower risk of having problems with the cord; and he's not too big, so he's not going to get stuck. I'm happy with the position he's in, with his head nicely tucked forward—so, yes, we can do this.' He smiled. 'As I said yesterday, I believe in keeping things natural as far as possible, so I'm not immediately going to say you'll have to have an episiotomy and forceps to help you deliver. It might end up that way, but we'll do our best to help you have the birth you want. Though I do want to remind you that if your labour doesn't progress, any delays mean that the baby's likely to be in distress and you'll need to have a section. No heroics, OK?'

'Agreed,' Ian Harris said firmly.

'Agreed,' Mrs Harris said, though she didn't sound quite so sure.

Ellis smiled at Ruby. 'Dilation?'

'Three centimetres.'

'OK. It's going to be a while yet before your baby arrives, so I'd suggest walking about a bit—the gravity will help him move down,' Ellis said.

'Would you mind very much if Coral—the trainee midwife you met yesterday—and one of the junior doctors came in to observe?' Ruby asked.

'No, that's fine,' Mrs Harris said. She squeezed her husband's hand. 'We're going to have our baby today, Ian. I can't believe it.'

It was a couple more hours before Mrs Harris was ready to start delivering the baby. Coral, the trainee midwife, and Lance, the new first-year doctor, came in to observe and Ruby introduced them both to the Harrises.

'Being on your elbows and knees will be the most comfortable position for you, as well as being the most effective position for delivering the baby, because you can move about a bit,' Ruby said. 'And resting on your elbows rather than your hands will protect your wrists.'

'Unless you really want an epidural, I'd recommend having either gas and air or pethidine as pain relief,' Ellis added, 'because an epidural will slow everything down.'

'I don't want a section,' Mrs Harris said, 'so I'll manage with gas and air.'

'Good on you,' Ellis said.

'The main thing to remember about a breech birth,' Ruby explained to Coral and Lance, 'is that you keep your hands off and be patient—you don't want the mum clenching her muscles if you touch her.'

'You intervene only if it's clear that the baby needs help,' Ellis said. 'Which is why we're using a foetal monitor to keep an eye on his heart rate.'

Ruby encouraged Mrs Harris to breathe through the contractions.

'I can see the baby now,' she said at last. 'When you have the next contraction, I want you to give a nice big push for me.'

The baby's buttocks arrived first, and then with the next contraction and the next push the back and shoulders were visible.

Ruby glanced at Ellis. As always when she delivered a baby with him, she noticed that he was almost misty-eyed. Ruby was, too; the moment a new life came into the world was so very special, and it was such a privilege to share it.

And Ellis was a particularly good doctor to work with; he was supportive, he listened to both the mum and the midwifery team, and he didn't try to rush any of the mums straight to Theatre at the first sign of a complication.

At the next push, the baby's legs came down.

'Well done,' Ruby said. 'You're doing just great. His legs are down, now. Keep breathing for me.'

The baby's shoulders and arms came out next, and

then Ruby glanced again at Ellis. At his nod, she moved into position, ready to catch the baby.

'Almost here. Next contraction, give me the biggest push you can. Scream if you need to. Shout. Whatever you want to do, that's fine. Just push,' she said.

And finally, the baby's head emerged.

'The baby's not crying,' Mr Harris said, looking panicky.

And the baby was blue. At a first glance, Ruby would give him an Apgar score of four—very low.

'It's fine,' Ellis reassured Mr Harris. 'I know right now this looks very scary, but this is totally normal for a breech birth. Do you want to cut the umbilical cord, and then we can get this little one warmed up a bit and ready for a cuddle?'

Thankfully it was enough to distract Mr Harris; Ruby swiftly clamped the cord and Ellis gave the scissors to Mr Harris to cut the cord while Ruby wrapped the baby in a warm towel.

Ruby then took the baby over to the warming tray for warm air to be blown on him.

'Do you want me to sort out the baby while you deliver the placenta?' Ellis asked.

She smiled at him. 'Yes, please.'

By the time she'd delivered the placenta, she was relieved to hear plenty of crying coming from Baby Harris, and she heard Ellis say, 'I'm pleased to say your little boy's pinked up very nicely indeed. He's got an Apgar score of nine.'

Ruby knew that last bit was aimed for her, and she felt the strain between her shoulders disappear. Everything was fine. And, better still, Ellis also hadn't mentioned anything about hip dysplasia, which could sometimes be a problem with breech babies.

Finally, Baby Harris was in his mum's arms, skin to skin, and took all of three sucks for his first feed before falling asleep.

Ruby examined Mrs Harris. 'I'm pleased to say that you don't need any stitches,' she said. 'You did absolutely brilliantly. Congratulations to both of you.'

'We could never have done it without you,' Mrs Harris said. 'I was so scared we'd have to just do what the doctor said.'

Ruby smiled. 'They're all pretty good here, actually.' She lowered her voice to a stage whisper. 'Though Ellis Webster is a bit special. But don't tell him I said that, or his head will swell so much that he won't be able to walk through the door for a week.'

Mrs Harris laughed.

'Let's get you settled down in the ward,' Ruby said, 'and you can get to know your baby.' She stroked the baby's cheek. 'He's beautiful.'

'Do you have children?' Mrs Harris asked.

'No.' She and Tom had thought very seriously about it, but then Tom had been diagnosed with leukaemia and it had never been the right time to discuss it again after that. 'Maybe one day,' she said wistfully.

And how odd that a picture flashed into her head. Of herself, tired yet glowing with happiness and holding a baby. And of Ellis sitting next to her, holding her hand and stroking the baby's head.

Ridiculous. And totally inappropriate.

Ellis was her friend, and *only* her friend. And she had a date lined up on Saturday night with a completely different man, the new registrar on her best friend's ward. She really shouldn't be thinking about that kind of thing.

Ellis didn't see Ruby over the weekend. He wanted to call her, but he knew she was going on a date with a colleague of Tina's. So he needed to back off. To give her a chance to get to know the guy and enjoy dating again.

Even though what he really wanted to do was to scoop her over his shoulder and carry her off to his lair.

Ridiculous. He knew that Ruby saw him only as a friend. So he was going to have to ignore this stupid antsy feeling. She deserved to feel happy again. It was just a pity it meant she'd find that happiness with another man rather than with him.

So on Monday lunchtime, he summoned his brightest smile when he saw her. 'Want to go grab a sandwich?'

'That'd be nice.'

He waited until they'd sat down in the canteen before he asked, 'So how was your date?'

'Fine.'

Her smile was a little too bright. 'But?' he asked.

She wrinkled her nose. 'He was a nice guy, but I don't think he was ready to date again yet.'

Was that Ruby's way of saying that she'd just discovered she wasn't ready to date again yet, too?

He battened down the hopes as she continued, 'I don't think he's quite over his divorce yet.'

'Ah. Baggage.'

She gave him a rueful smile. 'I guess we all have baggage when we get to this age.'

'Mmm.'

'Look at you,' she said softly.

Oh, no. He really didn't want to discuss that. He didn't like talking about his feelings. And he definitely didn't want to talk about his baggage. Ruby knew he was divorced, but he hadn't told her the whole messy story.

'Tom always said you'd never settle because you were trying to save people, to make up for the way they couldn't save your sister.'

'I guess that's part of it,' he said. 'Though I always wanted to be a doctor, even when Sally was still alive.' After Sally's death, he'd vowed to work abroad rather than stay in an English hospital, and it had caused a rift with his brothers; they couldn't understand why he risked himself the way he did, and they'd told him they didn't want to lose him the way they'd lost Sally. But, however much he'd tried to talk them round, he hadn't been able to make them see that he wanted to save all the other potential Sallys, and to do that it meant working abroad. 'And it's not why I became an obstetrician, either. I always planned to work in emergency medicine, like Tom. But then I did a rotation on the maternity ward and I fell in love with it—that special moment where you witness the miracle of a brand new life.'

'That's why I became a midwife, too,' she said softly. 'It never, ever gets old.'

'And it's even better in a world where things are sticky and you really feel that you need a miracle to happen and make things better. That first little cry...' Every time, it made him misty-eyed and glad to be alive, all at the same time.

'You still have itchy feet, don't you?' she asked. 'I know you're going back to the medical aid charity in a couple of months.'

'It's been arranged for a really long time,' Ellis said. And he did want to go back. The trouble was, he also wanted to stay in London. But he wasn't sure if he could—not if Ruby started dating someone else and it got serious. He'd promised Tom that he'd be there for Ruby, and he'd keep his promise; but he wasn't sure that his promise could stretch to watching her date another man and being happy about it. 'Anyway, we weren't talking about me,' he said, trying very hard to wriggle out of the subject. 'We were talking about your date.'

'I guess it was a case of nice guy, wrong time,' she said with a shrug.

'Would he be the right guy at a different time?' It was a bit like prodding a bruise, but Ellis wanted to know.

'Probably not,' she said. 'There wasn't that spark between us. Whereas the first time I saw Tom…'

'Yeah. I know.' He reached across and squeezed her hand briefly.

Mistake. Because every nerve-end in his own hand tingled at the contact.

He knew about sparks, all right. Ruby most definitely made him feel that spark. His feelings for anyone he'd dated before just paled by comparison—including his ex-wife. But Ruby was vulnerable, she was still missing Tom, and she was still probably not quite ready to move on. Adding his job to the mix…In his book, it all made her very firmly off limits.

'Hey. If you're not busy with a date at the weekend, maybe we could do something together,' he said lightly. 'There's that new action film.'

'You want me to go and see a guy-flick with you?' She laughed. 'Ellis, much as I love you…'

As a friend, he reminded himself sharply.

'....action flicks really aren't my favourites.'

'Hey, this one has a plot,' he protested.

'As if,' she scoffed, still laughing. 'All right, if you're so desperate to see it, I'll go with you. But it's on the understanding that I want ice cream *and* popcorn.'

'Deal,' he said. It wasn't a *date* date. But it would be enough. Because he didn't have the right to ask for more.

CHAPTER FOUR

IT WAS A busy week on the ward. Ruby's favourite day of the week was spent delivering twins in a birthing pool; the water birth was calm and peaceful, and it was a good experience for Coral, as well as being exactly what the mum wanted.

Saturday afternoon turned out to be dull and rainy, so she went to the cinema with Ellis to see the action flick. As promised, he bought her popcorn and ice cream; although the film wasn't really her cup of tea, she still enjoyed his company.

After going to a tiny bistro for pasta and a bottle of red wine, Ellis saw her home.

'Want to come in for some coffee?' she asked.

'I'd love to. Thanks.' He smiled at her.

When they were both sprawled comfortably on the sofa with a mug of coffee, Ruby said, 'Tina says I shouldn't give up on the dates just yet.'

'She's planning to set you up on a blind date with another of her colleagues?' Ellis asked.

'No. She suggested I try one of those online match-making sites.' She looked at him and raised an eyebrow. 'What, you don't approve?'

'It's not like going on a blind date with someone

who's a friend of a friend, which means you sort of know them already, or at least know that they're OK. With a dating site, you're planning to meet a total stranger,' Ellis said. 'And people don't always tell the truth on those things. They can put a photograph up that's years out of date and claim to like a lot of interesting things, just to get someone to pick them for a date.'

'Maybe the odd person would do that—odd in *both* senses of the word—but most people don't do that sort of thing. Don't be such a cynic. And think about it, Ellis. Once you're our age, most of your friends are in a relationship and so are most of their friends, which means you know hardly anyone else who's single. Apart from through friends or work, how else are you going to meet someone?'

'I guess you have a point,' he said.

She paused. 'Actually, you know, you could try it.'

'What?'

'Putting your profile on a dating site.'

'Why?' He looked at her in bewilderment.

'Because you haven't dated at all in the last year or so.'

'Yes, I have,' he protested.

'Here and there. Nothing serious.'

No. Because he didn't do serious relationships. Not since his divorce. He preferred to keep things light and uncomplicated, and he'd concentrated on his career rather than his love life. Not to mention the fact that he'd been fighting off inappropriate feelings towards Ruby for months. 'I've been busy,' he prevaricated.

'Ellis, you really don't have to put your life on hold for me,' she said gently.

He froze at her words. Did she *know*?

'I know Tom asked you to look after me, but that shouldn't be at the expense of your own happiness.'

He relaxed again. Clearly she was just thinking of his promise to Tom, and she didn't have a clue how he felt about her. Which was just as well. Because he didn't know how she felt about him—or if she could ever come to see him as anything more than her late husband's best friend. 'I'm fine as I am,' he said.

'But don't you get lonely, Ellis?'

'From time to time I do,' he admitted. 'But I have good friends and a job I love. That's enough for me.' And if he kept telling himself that, eventually he'd end up believing it.

At work on Tuesday morning, Ellis had a written request from the court. Something he really wasn't expecting. And something he really wanted to talk to Ruby about.

He went in search of her. 'Got a minute?' he asked. 'There's something I want to run by you.'

'Sorry, I've got wall to wall appointments this morning,' she said. 'And I'm running late. Can I come and grab you at lunchtime?'

'Sure—there's no immediate rush.'

Except at lunchtime Ellis had been called away to help at a difficult birth, and when he was on a break in the afternoon Ruby was in the middle of delivering a baby.

In the end he ended up meeting her after work for a drink.

'So what did you want to run by me?' she asked.

'I had a written request for information this morning,' he said. 'From the court.'

'The court?' She blinked. 'That sounds ominous.'

He shook his head. 'Nothing that should worry any-one in the department—it isn't a negligence case or any-thing. It's to do with a baby you and I delivered about a year ago—little Baby Edwards. Sadly, his parents have split up, and Billy Edwards wanted a paternity test.'

She grimaced. 'That's sad—and even sadder still be-cause it's probably not that unusual nowadays.'

'This case is definitely unusual,' he said. 'That's why the court wrote to me. The results came back and showed that Billy Edwards is the baby's father.'

Ruby looked puzzled. 'So if he's the father, which proves the paternity, why did the court write to you?'

'Because it turns out that Grace Edwards isn't the baby's mother.'

Her frown deepened. 'How come? Was she an IVF mum with a donated egg?'

'No. I looked up the paperwork today. Conception and pregnancy were all without any complications or intervention. Grace Edwards only had a section because the baby was getting distressed.'

'So if her former husband was definitely the father and the egg was hers, then surely Grace has to be the baby's mother? I mean, that's basic biology, Ellis.'

'You'd think so—but the genetic tests say not. And DNA doesn't lie.'

'Maybe there was an error in the tests?' she sug-gested.

He shook his head. 'They did a second set of DNA tests, just to make sure there wasn't some kind of error in the first set. The results show exactly the same thing: Baby Edwards is genetically related to Billy, but not to Grace.'

She blinked. 'This is surreal. How is that even possible, Ellis?'

'That,' he said dryly, 'is why the court's written to me. I'm going to discuss it with Theo Petrakis, but I wanted to talk to you first, to see if you remembered anything unusual about the birth.'

'No. I mean, I'd probably have to reread the paperwork to refresh my memory, because I can't remember every detail of every single baby I've ever delivered over the years.' She frowned. 'But I guess all midwives would remember births that have any out-of-the-ordinary features. I don't remember this one being an unusual case.'

'I'm going to have a chat with one of the genetic counsellors, too. Just to see if I'm missing something,' Ellis said. 'Because there definitely feels as if there's a piece of the puzzle missing. I just can't work out what.'

'Well, if you want a wing-woman, come and grab me,' she said.

Any time, he thought, but stopped himself before he said something stupid. 'Thanks.'

The following weekend, Ellis and Ruby were sitting on the balcony of his flat overlooking the park, enjoying the unseasonably mild evening and a bottle of wine.

'Tina was nagging me again this morning about signing up for the dating website,' Ruby said. She wrinkled her nose. 'Though I don't think I'll ever meet anyone who matches up to Tom.'

'Of course you won't, but it's still relatively early days,' Ellis said.

'So it's too soon to date again?'

'Only you can answer that,' he said. And even though he wanted to tell her to look right under her nose, he

was going to do the supportive thing. The *right* thing.
'We could always make a list of what you're looking
for from your perfect man.'

'You'd help me do that?'

'I guess Tina would probably be better at that than
I would,' he said.

'But you could give me feedback from a male point
of view—which my best friend, being female, can't,'
she pointed out.

'OK. Let's do it the old-fashioned way—pen and
paper, first.' He went into the living room and fetched
a notebook and pen. 'What do you want to do first?'

'My profile, I guess. How do I describe myself?'
she asked.

The most beautiful woman in the world. Not that
he was going to say that out loud. But with that elfin
crop and those huge blue eyes, she reminded him of
Audrey Hepburn. Though there was nothing fragile
and Holly Golightlyish about Ruby. She was strong.
Brave. Gorgeous.

He looked at her. 'Pretty, petite midwife?'

She groaned. 'No, because then I'll get all sleazy
stuff about men wanting naughty nurses in super-short
uniforms. I don't want to have to deal with that.'

'How about pretty, petite professional?' he suggested.

'And that's three Ps in a row—it looks wrong.'

He laughed. 'Make that four and add "picky".'

She laughed back. 'I guess.'

'I know. Pretty, petite medical professional seeks...'
He paused. 'So what are you looking for, Ruby?'

'Someone taller than me,' she said.

'That's not exactly difficult, given that you're all of
five foot two,' he teased.

She cuffed him. 'All right, we'll skip height. And, actually, looks aren't really that important.'

'So you don't want a guy who looks like a movie star?'

'Well, no woman with red blood in her veins is going to turn down a man who looks like Brad Pitt,' she said. 'But, seriously, it's personality that's more important.'

'Good sense of humour?'

'But not someone who does constant wisecracks— that'd drive me mad. And I don't like people who make someone else the butt of their humour all the time; I think that's mean-spirited.'

'Serious, then.'

'But with a nice smile and a sense of fun.'

'As I said, picky. Serious male with a nice smile and sense of fun.' He paused. 'Do you think you should add "professional" in there, too?'

'Could do.'

He wrote it down. 'What else?'

'Not a sports fiend. I don't want to spend my week-ends freezing cold at the side of a football pitch. Someone who likes films, a wide range of music and long walks.'

'OK. And what are you looking for? Friendship? Romance?'

'Both,' she said. 'I want to be friends as well as lovers.'

Yeah. *So did he.*

'Friendship leading to potential romance,' he said.

'You sound as if you've done this before. Or read a lot of personal ads.'

He smiled. 'I can assure you, I've never dated anyone through a personal ad. It's usually someone I've met through work.'

'But you haven't dated that much since I've known you.'

Partly because he didn't do serious relationships; and partly because he hadn't met anyone who made him feel even the slightest way that Ruby made him feel. It wasn't fair to date someone when you knew you couldn't give the relationship a real chance. When your heart was held elsewhere. 'I've been busy,' he said blandly.

'Maybe now's your chance to try it. We'll do your profile, next,' she said.

'Hey—I'm not planning to join a dating site,' he protested.

'Fair's fair,' she said. 'If I'm doing this, so are you. Hand over the pen and paper.'

He gave in.

'So. TDH doctor.'

'TDH?'

'Tall, dark and handsome.' She rolled her eyes. 'Come off it, Ellis. Even you must know that one.'

'Along with GSOH,' he deadpanned. 'What everyone says in their profile.'

'You're serious and deep,' she said.

He grimaced. 'Which makes me sound boring.'

'No, you do have a sense of fun—it's just that sometimes you need teasing out of your shell. Serious and deep,' she repeated, 'with principles.'

'And now I sound like a character from a Victorian novel. The one who doesn't get the girl because he's stuffy.'

'You're not stuffy, Ellis.' She grinned. 'Principles and dimples.'

'Dimples?' He looked at her, mystified.

'When you smile. You do know I've heard some of

the mums on the ward sigh over you? As well as all the female staff?'

'No, they don't.' He groaned. 'OK. We need to stop this, right now.'

She shook her head. 'Uh-uh. We're doing this. What are you looking for, Ellis?'

He could lie.

Or he could take a risk and tell her the truth.

'Someone bright and sparkly, to make my dimples come out,' he said softly.

'That's better,' she said. 'Vegetarian?'

'No, not necessarily,' he said. 'I'm looking for someone who enjoys food, films and walking by the sea.'

'For friendship leading to potential romance?'

'That sounds about right. So what do we have?' He shifted so they could both see the notepad, and flicked back to the page he'd written on.

'Pretty, petite medical professional seeks serious professional male with a nice smile and sense of fun, who likes films, music and long walks, for friendship leading to potential romance,' he read aloud.

She took the notebook from him and turned over to the next page.

'TDH doctor, serious and deep—with principles—seeks bright, sparkly female to make his dimples come out. Looking for foodie film-buff who enjoys seaside strolls, for friendship leading to potential romance.'

He groaned again. 'I hate that bit about the dimples. It sounds really pathetic.'

'Tough. It's staying. Your dimples are cute.' She flicked back to her list. 'You know, Ellis, this list could be describing you.'

His heart skipped a beat.

Was this the chance he'd been looking for? Was she telling him in her quiet, understated way, that she'd consider dating him?

'And my list,' he said softly, 'could be describing you.'

They looked at each other, and it felt as if the air was humming.

Should he make a move?

If he did and she reacted the wrong way, he could always blame the wine tomorrow morning, apologise profusely, and rescue their friendship.

And if he made a move and she reacted the right way...

'Maybe,' he said, 'neither of us needs to put an ad on the dating site.'

She didn't pull away or look horrified at the idea.

So he leaned forward and gave in to what he'd wanted to do for a year or more. He touched his mouth very lightly to hers.

CHAPTER FIVE

RUBY'S MOUTH TINGLED as Ellis's lips brushed hers very lightly. Warm. Sweet. Exploring rather than demanding. Gentle. Every kiss, every touch, made her want more.

She'd dreamed of this moment, but the reality was something else. Full of delight—and full of terror. Delight, because now she knew that the attraction she felt towards Ellis was mutual; but terror, because if this all went wrong she knew she'd lose him from her life, and she didn't have the strength to cope with losing anyone else right now.

When he broke the kiss and drew back, his eyes were dark. With worry, guilt or both? she wondered. Because she couldn't tell a thing from his expression. And she was racked with panic.

'Sorry. I shouldn't have done that. I…' He broke off with a grimace.

'No.' She reached across and took his hand. 'Ellis. You and I…we're friends.'

'Yes. Of course.'

'I like being with you,' she said carefully.

'Uh-huh.'

Now he sounded as if he'd gone into polite and neutral mode. So did he think this was a mistake? Or was he worried that she thought it was a mistake? Maybe she needed to take the risk and be totally honest with him.

'You tick every box on my list. But if I date you...' She took a deep breath. 'It scares me, Ellis. You don't tend to date women very often, and when you do the relationship doesn't last for very long. And you're going back to the medical aid charity in a couple of months.'

'For a month's assignment, yes,' he confirmed. 'As you know, I'm helping to set up a new medical centre in Zimbabwe.'

'But isn't that...' She looked at him wide-eyed. There was so much unrest in the country. It was a huge risk.

As if he guessed what she was thinking, he said quietly, 'It's an area that's fairly remote and really in need of help. Especially obstetrics. There are so few medics, and so many fatalities that could easily be prevented.'

Which she knew was a huge draw for him. Even though he'd said he hadn't become an obstetrician for his sister's sake, she knew that he wanted to make a difference, the way someone should've made a difference for her. Of course he needed to be there.

But was he going just to set it up? Or would he stay for a few months after that?

'And what happens after your month's assignment?' she asked.

'I don't actually have an answer for that right now,' he admitted.

Ruby said nothing, but Ellis could see the worry in her eyes. She was clearly thinking that if he dated her, she was going to end up being hurt when he left.

Hurting her was the last thing he'd ever want to do. And even though right now he really wanted to kiss her again—kiss her until they both forgot the world outside—he knew he had to do the decent thing. The unselfish thing.

'OK. Let's forget all about this and stick to being just friends,' he said.

'Yes. No.' She shook her head. 'I don't know. I wasn't expecting this.'

'I'm sorry.'

'I'm not. And I am. And...' She grimaced. 'I'm not making any sense at all, am I?'

'No, you're not,' he agreed, and she noticed the slightest glint of humour in his eyes. Though she knew he was laughing with her rather than at her.

Time for another burst of honesty, perhaps, she thought. 'I wanted you to kiss me just now,' she told him.

His face was completely inscrutable now, and she had no idea whether she was fixing a problem or making things even more of a mess.

'But, at the same time, it scares me. I can't afford to lose you from my life, Ellis. And your relationships never last for very long. You said yourself that you've never settled for anyone, not even your ex-wife—and you're going away again soon and you don't really know if you're coming back.'

'I haven't settled down because I've never met anyone who really made me want to settle down, not in the long term,' he said.

She hadn't pushed him about the details of his marriage, though he'd made it very clear when they'd talked in the past that he wasn't still in love with his ex. But when he said he'd never met anyone who made him want to settle, did that also include her? Ruby wondered.

Or could she be the one who could make him feel differently about settling down?

'Plus you're Tom's best friend,' she said. 'And I feel guilty.'

'Did you feel guilty about dating Tina's colleague?' he asked.

'No,' she admitted.

'So what's the difference between dating him and dating me?'

'Because I know you.' Because Ellis *mattered*—though she didn't quite want to admit that. And because the world needed people like Ellis, people who were prepared to be selfless and make a difference. Asking him to stay would be so selfish of her.

'You could,' he said, 'pretend that you don't know me. Pretend that I'd just answered your ad.'

She was still holding his hand; he rubbed his thumb gently against her palm. 'Ruby. You said you wanted to date again. But at the same time it scares you, right?'

'Right,' she admitted.

'Because you're worried it will go wrong?'

If he'd asked her the question about anyone else, she would've said no. But where Ellis was concerned, she worried that it would go wrong. That she'd lose him back to the medical aid charity—that his month's assignment would turn into two, then six, then a year... That he'd quietly vanish from her life, just as quietly as he'd walked in and become her rock when Tom was diagnosed with leukaemia. Leaving her lonely again. And feeling guilty for feeling lonely, because she knew what he did was important, and in the scheme of things her loneliness was the proverbial hill of beans.

'I don't know,' she said, feeling more confused than she had in a long time.

'What shift are you on, on Friday?' he asked.

'Early.'

'Then why don't we give it a try on Friday evening?' he suggested.

'Have an actual date, you mean?'

'Uh-huh.'

She took a deep breath. 'Doing what exactly?'

'Dinner, maybe. Dancing. Whatever you'd like to do.'

Would there be more kissing? Her body flooded with heat at the idea.

'Ruby?' he asked softly.

Could she be brave and take the risk—date the man she'd started to think of as more than just a friend? And could she squash the guilt she felt about dating again? She swallowed hard. 'Provided we go Dutch, OK.'

'No. If I ask someone out to dinner, that means I'm paying,' he said firmly. 'And there aren't any strings attached, if that's what you're worrying about. Dinner is just dinner. End of.'

'Then do I get to pay next time? To keep it fair?'

He frowned. 'I'm more than happy to pay for your dinner, Ruby. I'm not expecting you to...' He blew out a breath. 'Well. That's not how I operate.'

She knew what he wasn't saying. He wasn't expecting her to sleep with him in exchange for her dinner. The problem was...she did want to sleep with him. And that made her feel even more awkward and guilty. What was wrong with her? Was it just that it had been a while since she'd been physically sated? Was this some crazy hormonal thing? Or was it more than that? The whole thing left her feeling like a confused mess. 'I guess.'

'So will you have dinner with me on Friday, Ruby?' he asked softly.

'I...'

'We'll take it light and easy. We dress up a bit, eat nice food, drink lovely wine, then maybe go dancing if you'd like to.'

It sounded so good. Everything she wanted. But did she want more from this relationship than he did? And why was she so drawn to Ellis anyway—when she knew he loved his job working abroad, always on the move, and she wanted something different? If she looked at it sensibly, Ellis was the last person she should date. He didn't want the same things out of life that she did. He'd been brilliant, a total rock since he'd come back to London for Tom, but she knew he couldn't put his life on hold for ever. That wouldn't be fair. And their real lifestyles weren't compatible, with him moving on all the time and her staying in the same place.

To cover her confusion and her worries, she asked, 'Can you even dance?'

'That's for me to know,' he said, 'and you to find out. Provided you wear high heels and lipstick.' He brought her hand up to his mouth and kissed the back of her fingers, looking her straight in the eyes as he did so. And it sent desire licking all the way down her spine. How had she never noticed before just how hot Ellis was?

'Friday,' he said. 'I'll pick you up at seven. And I'll see you at work tomorrow.'

Dating Ellis.

The very idea put Ruby into a flat spin.

And she couldn't get those kisses out of her head.

The way his mouth had felt against her skin…Her whole body tingled at the memory.

She still couldn't quite believe that she'd agreed to this. And, worse still, that she'd actually told him she was attracted to him and he ticked all the boxes on her wish list for a partner.

He should have run a mile. Especially given that he didn't date much and his relationships never lasted long. And, given that he was planning to leave England again in a couple of months and he wasn't totally sure that he was coming back, he shouldn't be interested in her. He should've brushed everything aside.

But he hadn't.

He'd actually asked her out.

And he'd said that she fitted his wish list, too.

This could be perfect. Happiness she'd never expected to find again—and with a man Tom would most definitely approve of, because he'd loved Ellis like a brother.

Yet it could also be the worst mistake she'd ever made. How awkward would it make things at work if things went wrong between them? He wasn't just her friend, he was one of the colleagues she liked working with most.

And what would happen when he left? Could they make a go of a long-distance relationship, or could they find some sort of compromise? Or would it end up being a total mess?

She was going to have to be very, very careful.

In the middle of a busy morning on the ward, Ellis got a call from one of the ultrasonographers. 'Ellis, can I have a second opinion?'

'Sure. What's the problem?'

'I'm not happy with the baby I'm scanning right now. I think the baby's showing signs of anaemia—the blood flow's a bit too quick for my liking.'

Ellis knew that meant the baby's blood was likely to be thinner, with fewer red blood cells—and that might mean the need for surgical intervention to correct the anaemia. 'How old is the baby, and who's the mum's midwife?' he asked.

'The baby's twenty-six weeks, and the midwife's Ruby.'

The best person he could've hoped for. She always developed a real rapport with her mums. Ellis loved working with her—which was probably the best reason for him not to date her and risk that working relationship. He pushed the thought away. 'OK. I'm coming now, and I'll see if I can get Ruby to come with me.'

She was in the middle of a consultation, but agreed to come along as soon as she was done.

The ultrasonographer introduced him quickly to Mrs Perkins. 'Dr Webster's just come along to give me a second opinion,' she explained.

As soon as Ellis looked at the screen, he agreed with her assessment: the baby's blood flow was definitely too quick.

'Is something wrong with my baby?' Mrs Perkins asked, looking worried.

'At the moment it's just a precaution, so try not to worry,' he said. 'It might be that the baby's a little bit anaemic, but we can to do something to sort that out. Do you mind if I look at your notes?'

As soon as Ellis saw Mrs Perkins's blood group, he had a pretty good idea of what the problem was. 'Your blood group's rhesus negative,' he said. 'And I can see here that you've been having anti-D injections.'

She nodded. 'They're not the nicest things in the world, but it's worth it to keep the baby safe.'

Clearly it had been explained to her that if the baby's blood group was rhesus positive, her body would develop antibodies that would cross the placenta and attack the baby's red blood cells, causing anaemia. Injections of anti-D would stop her body developing antibodies.

Except, by the look of it, the anti-D hadn't worked. So there was a little more to this than met the eye.

'And your husband's blood group is rhesus positive?' he asked.

She nodded. 'That's why they said I had to have the anti-D, because the baby's blood was likely to be rhesus positive as well.'

At that point, Ruby came in. 'Hello, Helen.' She smiled at Mrs Perkins and squeezed her hand. 'How are you doing?'

'I'm fine, but they think my baby's anaemic.' Mrs Perkins bit her lip. 'And I had all the anti-D injections. I didn't miss a single one.'

'I know.'

'There is one circumstance where the anti-D doesn't work,' Ellis said quietly, coming to sit on her other side. 'I apologise in advance if this brings back any bad memories, and I know your notes say that this is your first baby, but have you ever been pregnant before?'

'I don't think so,' Mrs Perkins said.

'It might be possible,' Ruby said gently, 'that you didn't realise you were pregnant—that maybe your period was a bit late and you put it down to stress, and then your period was heavier than normal.'

'I...' Mrs Perkins shook her head, and a tear trickled down her cheek. 'This is so stupid. I can't remember.'

'It could have been a long time ago,' Ellis said. 'But it's really common for women to be pregnant, not realise it, and lose the baby before they have any idea they might be pregnant. If that happened to you, it's very possible that your body was already sensitised to the antibodies, so the anti-D wouldn't work for you.'

'So it's my fault the baby's anaemic?'

'Not at all,' he reassured her, squeezing her hand. 'You did everything by the book. It's just one of these things. But I would like to do some more tests, Mrs Perkins. I'd like to take a blood sample from the baby.'

'How does that work?' she asked.

'I take a tiny, tiny sample from the baby with a needle—it's not so nice for you, because it means putting a needle through your abdomen into your womb,' he said. 'The same way an amniocentesis is done.'

She shook her head. 'It doesn't matter about me. I just want the baby to be all right.'

'I promise you, we're going to keep a close eye on you so you don't have to worry,' Ruby said.

'We can do the sample right here, right now—or we can wait for someone to come and be with you, if you'd rather,' Ellis said.

'I want Joe,' Mrs Perkins said. 'My husband. He was supposed to be here for the scan, but there was an emergency at work and he got called in.' Another tear trickled down her cheek. 'Or am I putting the baby at risk by waiting?'

Ruby put an arm round her shoulders and hugged

her, and Ellis handed her a tissue. 'No, you're not. It's absolutely fine to wait until your husband can be here before we do the blood test,' he reassured her.

'What happens if the baby's anaemic?'

'I don't want to frighten you, but severe anaemia can cause the baby's heart to fail, or even mean that you have a stillbirth,' he said gently. 'But we can tell how much of a problem the anaemia is from that blood sample, and if necessary we can give the baby a blood transfusion.'

Mrs Perkins looked shocked. 'You mean I'll have the baby today? But I'm only twenty-six weeks! That's...' She shook her head. 'Surely I can't have the baby now?'

'No, you won't be having the baby today. I mean we can do a transfusion through a needle while the baby's still in your womb,' Ellis explained gently. 'We'll do it under a local anaesthetic so you won't feel it, but it does mean you'll need to stay in overnight, and we'll need to do this every couple of weeks until the baby's born. But the transfusions will stop the anaemia.'

'I'll call Joe for you, shall I?' Ruby asked.

Mrs Perkins nodded. 'But if the baby's anaemic, how come I didn't feel any different? And I've made sure I've eaten plenty of leafy green veg, and I eat lean red meat twice a week.'

'It's honestly not anything you've done,' Ellis reassured her. 'And that diet sounds about perfect for you and the baby. Try not to worry. And I'll see you a bit later this afternoon, OK?'

The baby's blood sample showed a worrying level of anaemia, so Ellis and Ruby went to see Mr and Mrs Perkins.

'Is our baby all right?' Mrs Perkins asked.

'The sample says the baby's anaemic, but as I explained earlier, a blood transfusion will fix that,' Ellis said.

'So the baby gets a transfusion while still inside Helen?' Mr Perkins asked. 'Isn't that dangerous?'

'It's invasive, yes, and you're right that the procedure gives a very small risk of miscarriage or early labour,' Ruby said.

'What if the baby doesn't have the transfusion?' Mr Perkins asked.

'Then the anaemia will get worse and it could cause other problems.'

'Such as?' Mr Perkins asked.

'The baby might develop heart problems. And I'm sorry to say that, in the worst case scenario, the baby could be stillborn.'

Mr Perkins went white.

'My advice is that, although it's an invasive treatment, the baby needs the blood transfusion, and the advantages outweigh the risks,' Ellis said gently.

'If we say yes, how does it work?' Mrs Perkins asked.

'We'll give you a local anaesthetic to numb the area so you won't feel it,' Ellis said. 'And we'll give you a sedative to relax you, plus a sedative to the baby to make sure that the baby doesn't move during the procedure.'

'That means you won't feel the baby moving for a little while afterwards,' Ruby said, 'but that's perfectly normal and the sedative will wear off for both of you within a couple of hours.'

'We'll do an ultrasound scan to show us where the baby is,' Ellis continued, 'and then we'll give the baby a few millilitres of blood through a needle in the umbilical cord—that means the blood's absorbed better.'

'And it's a one-off?' Mrs Perkins asked.

'We'll give you weekly scans from now on,' Ellis said, 'to see how the baby's doing—but it's quite likely that the baby will need a transfusion every two to four weeks until birth.'

Mr Perkins looked at them, wide-eyed. 'Whose blood does the baby get?'

'It's donated blood, fully screened—type O rhesus positive,' Ellis said.

'I'm O positive. Can I give the blood?' Mr Perkins asked.

'I'll check with the haematologist, and you'll need to have some tests before they can say yes, but if it's OK with the haem team then it's more than fine by me,' Ellis said. 'From now on you'll be under my care and Ruby's, so you'll always see us when you come to the hospital—and if you ever have any worries at any time, I want you to ring us or come and see us, OK? Because that's what we're here for—to look after you and to reassure you if you're concerned about anything, no matter how small it might seem.'

'OK. We'll do it.' Mrs Perkins bit her lip. 'When does the first one happen?'

'Today,' Ellis said. 'And I'd like you to stay in overnight, just so we can keep an eye on you.'

'I agree,' Mr Perkins said. 'If anything happens, Helen, you'll be in the right place.'

'But the chances of anything happening are really, really small,' Ellis reassured them. 'Is there anyone you need to call?'

'No—but can I stay with Helen while it's being done?' Mr Perkins asked.

'Of course you can,' Ruby said.

To Ellis's relief, the haematology tests meant that Mr Perkins was able to donate the blood. The procedure only took a couple of minutes, and he and Ruby talked the Perkinses through every single step, making sure they could see the baby on the screen and pointing out the baby's heart beating to reassure them that the sedative wasn't a problem.

'As Ruby said earlier, it takes up to three hours for the sedative to wear off,' Ellis reminded them afterwards. 'Don't worry if you don't feel the baby moving for a little while. I'm going to prescribe antibiotics to make sure you don't get any infection. But if you feel hot or any kind of pain, or there's any redness or bleeding around the area where I injected you, tell the nursing staff straight away, OK? And I'll be in to see you later.'

'Now that's something you couldn't have done in the middle of a field or an earthquake,' Ruby said to Ellis softly when Helen Perkins had gone up to the ward to settle in. 'And you loved every second of it, didn't you?'

'Cutting edge stuff, you mean? Yes, I did,' he admitted. 'What I like most is being able to make a real difference.'

And now he'd seen that he could make a real difference working in a London hospital just as easily as he could working for a medical aid charity, Ruby hoped that would mean he was more likely to come back to London after his assignment.

'Are you still OK for Friday?' he asked.

She nodded. 'I'm still OK.'

'Good.'

To her shock, he leaned over and kissed her swiftly on the mouth.

'Ellis!' she said.

'Just checking,' he said softly. 'See you later. I want to go and make sure that Helen Perkins has settled in OK.'

And she'd just bet he'd ring in later that evening when he was off duty, just to make sure. It was the kind of man he was. A good man, one who cared deeply.

But the idea of actually dating him still thrilled her and terrified her in equal measures. It could be oh, so good between them. But what if his month's assignment made him realise how much he loved moving on? What if his itchy feet came back? Would he expect her to go with him? She didn't want to leave the London Victoria; she loved her job here. Yet she also knew that Ellis loved his freedom. So one of them would have to make a sacrifice. She didn't want Ellis to have regrets or feel trapped because of her; that wasn't fair. If he came back after his assignment, it had to be because he wanted to be with her, not because he felt any obligation towards her or to Tom. Ruby didn't want Ellis to give up everything for her sake, and she had a feeling that Ellis wouldn't want to make her give up everything for his sake, either.

So maybe she should call off the date. Push the attraction to one side and be sensible. Find someone else—someone who was quite happy to stay in London.

The problem was, the attraction between them was growing stronger by the day. Especially since she'd discovered that it was mutual and that Ellis didn't think of her as just a friend.

Maybe, then, she should just stop thinking. Let it happen. And hope that it was going to work out.

CHAPTER SIX

RUBY WAS GLAD of a super-busy day on Friday so she didn't have time to think about her date with Ellis that evening.

When she got home after her shift, she spent ages working out what to wear.

He'd said high heels and lipstick. Which meant dressing up. She tried on every dress in her wardrobe, and in the end she opted for her favourite little black dress, teamed with high heels.

She'd just finished doing her make-up when the doorbell went. She glanced at her watch. Dead on seven. So it wasn't a neighbour or an unexpected delivery; it was Ellis.

A shiver ran down her spine. She felt ridiculously nervous. There was no reason for it: this was Tom's best friend, a man she'd known for eighteen months and who'd been there for her at her darkest hour. A man she knew she could rely on. So she shouldn't be in the slightest bit edgy about seeing him.

Yet tonight was different—their first date—and it felt as if butterflies were doing a stampede in her stomach.

She opened the door. He looked breathtakingly

handsome in a dark suit, crisp white shirt and silk tie. His smile was slightly shy as he handed her a bouquet of pink roses.

'I thought red ones might be a bit over the top,' he said.

She smiled back at him. 'Thank you, Ellis. They're beautiful. I'll just put them in water. Come in.'

'You look lovely.'

Was it her imagination or did he sound as nervous as she felt?

He bent his head to kiss her cheek, and somehow they ended up clashing heads.

He gave her a rueful look. 'Sorry. I didn't mean to hurt you. I, um...' His voice faded, as if he didn't have a clue what to say to her.

'It's fine,' she reassured him. More than fine, because it told her that he was just as nervous about this as she was.

As she found a vase and put the flowers in water, he leaned against the kitchen worktop. 'I've booked dinner at a place not too far from here. It's a nice evening, so would you like to walk or shall I call a taxi?' Then he glanced at her shoes. 'Ah. Scratch that. I'll call a taxi.'

'Well, you did tell me to wear high heels,' she reminded him with a smile. 'But no, you're right. It's a nice evening, so we can walk. Let me grab a pair of flatter shoes, and I'll change into these ones again when we get there.'

On the way to the restaurant, his hand bumped against hers a couple of times. When she didn't pull away, the next time he caught her fingers in his, and held her hand the rest of the way to the restaurant. It was the lightest, sweetest contact: and it sent a tingle all the way through her.

Though it also put her head in a spin and she didn't have a clue what to say to Ellis. On a normal night, she would have chatted away to him about everything under the sun; but tonight she had to resort to talking about work. 'I hope Helen Perkins is getting on OK.'

'I'm sure she is. It's worrying for parents, though, when something like that happens.' He grimaced. 'I have a feeling this might be one of the rare cases when I suggest an early section, for the baby's sake.'

'I'll back you,' she said. 'Better to be slightly disappointed at not sticking to your birth plan, than to be... Well.' They both knew what the worst-case scenario was in cases of foetal anaemia. The kind of birth that broke her heart because it felt as if all the light in the world had just gone out, and there was nothing you could do to make the loss easier on the parents.

'Yeah,' he said heavily.

When they got to the restaurant, Ruby changed her shoes and handed her bag and coat in at the cloakroom. But, on the way to their table, she tripped. To her horror, she heard a snap and when her foot wobbled she had to grab Ellis's arm to stop herself falling flat on her face. Clearly she'd just broken the heel of her shoe.

'It's just as well we walked so I have another pair of shoes with me,' she said wryly. 'I'll go back to the cloakroom and get them.'

'I'm sorry,' he said.

'It's not your fault. It's me being clumsy. I'm sorry. Don't wait for me. I'll join you at our table.' She slipped off her shoes and walked barefoot back to the cloakroom. So much for dressing up. And those heels had been her favourite pair, glamorous black patent leather which actually managed to be comfortable as well as pretty.

She tried her best to push the disappointment aside and joined Ellis in the restaurant.

Once they'd ordered their food and a bottle of New Zealand Sauvignon Blanc, it was Ellis's turn to be clumsy. He leaned over to top up her glass of wine, and ended up knocking it all over the table. The tablecloth was soaked, and some of the wine landed in her lap.

'Oh, no.' He looked horrified. 'I'm so sorry.'

'It's OK. It'll soon dry off. Anyway, it's white wine so it'll come out in the wash. It's not as if you spilled red wine over a cream lacy dress or something.' She smiled at him. 'I think that makes us one-all in the clumsy stakes tonight.'

'I guess so,' he said wryly, 'but I *am* sorry, Rubes. This was meant to be a nice evening out.'

And so far it had pretty much been a disaster. Anything that could've gone wrong had actually gone wrong. 'It doesn't matter,' she reassured him.

The waiter changed the tablecloth for them and reset the table, but he didn't look pleased about the extra work or try to make conversation with them as he sorted out the table. And then it seemed an endless wait for their meal to arrive; Ruby noticed that people who'd been seated after them had already been served with their food—which was odd, because she and Ellis had both ordered something simple, not something that would take a huge amount of preparation or a long time to cook.

Ellis was clearly thinking the same thing, because he said, 'I wonder if they've forgotten us?'

Though they couldn't ask because there wasn't a waiter to be seen in the dining room.

'I'll go and find someone,' he said. 'Back in a tick.'

He came back looking apologetic. 'It seems our order slipped off the pile. They're sorting us out now.'

'Never mind,' she said brightly.

And when the food finally came, Ruby didn't have the heart to tell Ellis that her chicken was tough and her vegetables were soggy. Though, from the way he picked at his food, she was pretty sure that the meal he'd chosen was just as badly cooked.

'Would you like a dessert and coffee?' he asked politely.

'Thank you, but I think I'll pass,' she said.

'Me, too,' he said. 'I'll get the bill.'

The bill took an excruciatingly long time to come, but eventually Ellis managed to pay for their meal.

This had to be the worst date ever.

So much for sharing a nice dinner out and then going dancing. The food had been awful, the service had been worse, and as Ruby had broken the heel on her shoe he didn't want to suggest dancing and make her feel awkward.

And he didn't have a clue what to say to her as he walked her home. Which was crazy, because he'd always been able to talk to Ruby.

Maybe this was a sign, he thought, that they shouldn't do this. The last thing he wanted to do was to end up hurting her when things went wrong between them, the way his marriage had imploded. She deserved better than that.

'Would you like to come in for coffee?' she asked when they reached her front door.

On a normal evening he would've said yes and spent time chatting to her. Tonight, he just wanted to go home before something else happened to increase the strain between them. 'No, I'd better let you get on,' he said.

'Well, thanks for this evening,' she said with a bright, bright smile.

Ellis knew she was being polite, because it had been truly awful. Even the dates of his teens hadn't been this bad. 'Pleasure,' he said, even though it hadn't been.

He didn't kiss her goodbye, not even on the cheek; he just gave her an awkward smile, waited until she'd let herself in, and left.

And he was still feeling bad by the time he'd walked home. In the end, he gave in and texted her. *I'm so sorry about tonight. It was a total disaster.*

His phone beeped almost immediately with a reply. *Not your fault.*

Wasn't it? The problem with her shoe wasn't his fault—but the restaurant most definitely was. He should've checked the online reviews first, because they would've highlighted that the food was awful and so was the service.

His phone beeped again. *If you were as nervous as I was, I think it all went wrong because we both tried too hard.*

Nervous?

Yeah. He'd been nervous, all right. Worried that he was going to mess everything up. Clearly she'd felt the same. And he'd barely managed a proper conversation with her. They'd ended up talking shop. How pathetic was that? He knew he could talk to Ruby about anything under the sun. They didn't need to rely on awkward conversations about work.

Time to put it right. He picked up the phone and called her.

'Hey, Ellis.'

'Hey, yourself. You're right, Rubes. I was nervous, too. Which is stupid, because we've known each other for so long.'

'I guess.'

'If we'd just gone out together as we normally do—' as friends, though he didn't say it '—we would have laughed it all off. But you're right. Because it was a date, we had all these expectations of what it ought to be like, and I guess we made it difficult for ourselves.'

'Uh-huh.' Her voice was expressionless.

'Maybe,' he said, 'we could try again. But this time we should keep it simple and take the pressure off.'

'What do you have in mind?'

Pretty much what they'd talked about when they'd made those ridiculous lists for that dating site. 'I'm working a late shift tomorrow, but I thought we could have a walk somewhere nice on Sunday morning, if you're off duty—and also depending on the weather, because it's not going to be much fun if it's bucketing down with rain. And then we can find somewhere to grab lunch.'

'That sounds great,' she said. 'What time?'

'Meet you at yours at ten? Oh, and no high heels.'

She laughed. 'Definitely not, if we're going for a walk. OK. See you then.'

Ellis felt a lot better by the time he rang off. And better still when Sunday dawned bright and sunny—a perfect late September morning, with a blue sky and the sun burnishing the bronze, reds and golds of the autumn leaves.

He rang her doorbell and waited for her to answer.

This time when he kissed her cheek, there was no clash of heads, no awkwardness. It felt *right*. He could smell the soft floral scent she wore and his mouth tingled where it touched her skin.

She'd looked gorgeous in high heels and a little black dress on Friday night, but she looked just as gorgeous this morning in faded jeans, a blue silky long-sleeved top that brought out the colour of her eyes, and flat walking shoes. A pocket Venus, Ellis thought, all curves that he wanted to gather closer—but he'd try and take it easy today.

They caught the Tube through to Kew, where Ruby insisted on paying for their tickets to the gardens. 'You bought dinner on Friday, so I'm paying. No arguments.'

'Only on condition that you let me buy you lunch,' he said.

'That's a deal,' she said with a smile.

He enjoyed waking through the gardens with her to the Arboretum, where they explored the treetop walkway. His hand brushed against hers several times and then her fingers curled round his; the light contact made him feel all warm inside. This felt so much more natural than their posh date on Friday night. Maybe, just maybe, they could get this thing to work.

They stopped in one of the cafés for a lunch of hot soup, artisan bread and cheese. It was much simpler than Friday's food, but came with much better service; this time, he relaxed with her and could enjoy her company instead of worrying what would go wrong next.

They wandered through the glasshouses together, hand in hand, then headed back outside to crunch through the fallen leaves. Ellis found a conker fresh out of its shell beneath the chestnut tree and presented it to Ruby with a smile. 'It's the same colour as your hair.'

'Thank you. That's very poetic, Ellis.' She smiled back at him and put the conker safely in her pocket.

That smile undid him. He couldn't resist pulling her into his arms and dipping his head to kiss her. He brushed his lips lightly against hers, once, twice; then she caught his lower lip gently between hers.

Odd how a single kiss could put his head into such a spin.

He wrapped his arms more tightly round her, and her arms were wrapped round his neck, holding him just as tightly. His eyes closed as she let him deepen the kiss, and it felt as if the late afternoon sunshine was filling his soul.

When he broke the kiss, her pupils were huge and there was a slash of colour across her cheekbones. He wanted to tell her how beautiful she looked, but the words felt flat and not enough, so he stole a last kiss and hoped she'd guess what was in his head.

Finally, when the light started to fade, they headed back on the Tube to her flat.

'I'm not ready for today to end just yet,' Ruby said on her doorstep. 'Will you stay for dinner?'

'I'd like that. I can be your sous-chef, if you want.' He knew his way around Ruby's kitchen; he'd cooked quite a few meals there towards the end of Tom's illness, to give Ruby a break and make sure that both she and Tom had something nutritious to eat to keep their strength up.

'That sounds good to me.' She rummaged through the cupboards, found a bottle of white wine and held it so he could see the label. 'I know it's not chilled, but is this OK?'

'More than OK,' he said with a smile. 'And this time I'll try not to knock my glass over.' Funny, it was easy to laugh about their disastrous date now. At the time, he'd been mortified and felt as gauche as a teenager, but he had a feeling that this was going to become a favourite story for both of them in years to come: the night of the Worst Date Ever.

'Is risotto OK with you?' she asked.

'More than OK—I love risotto,' he said.

She poured them both a glass of wine, and Ellis chopped the vegetables while she made the base for the risotto. Working with her in the kitchen felt as natural as working together at the hospital. As if this was meant to be...

They ate at the kitchen table, and it was perfect. The right food, the right company, the right ambience. Especially as Ruby produced posh ice cream for pudding, and even posher shortbread to go with it.

'Today's been really lovely,' she said when they'd finished eating and done the washing up.

'I've enjoyed it, too. I'd better let you get on, though.' He'd taken up the whole of her day already. Any more would be greedy.

'I'm not actually doing a lot—all I plan to do is curl up on the sofa and watch that dance competition show on the television,' she said. 'You're very welcome to stay and join me, if you don't have anything better to do.'

How could he resist?

Especially when they ended up sitting with her on his lap and his arms wrapped round her.

'So which is your favourite kind of dancing, ballroom or Latin?' he asked.

'Ballroom, I think. I love it when the woman is dressed like a princess and they dance a dreamy waltz.' She laughed and sang a snatch of 'Moon River'.

'I didn't know you could sing,' he said, surprised.

'Not that well,' she said. 'I've got a limited vocal range. Tom says—*said*,' she corrected herself, 'that I only manage that one because Audrey Hepburn's vocal range was tiny, too, and "Moon River" was written especially for her to be able to sing it.'

'You remind me a bit of Audrey Hepburn,' Ellis said, tipping his head to one side. 'All pixie haircut and huge eyes. Well, except obviously your eyes are blue.'

Ruby looked pleased. 'She's one of my favourite actresses. I love her films—and Grace Kelly's.'

Ones with happy endings? That was something he couldn't guarantee for her. Not wanting to break the mood, he said nothing and just kept holding her.

The next dance was a waltz—but this time not the dreamy, princessy sort that Ruby had said she liked. It was a dark, edgy and sensual...

'That's amazing choreography.' Ruby fanned herself. 'Oh, to able to dance with someone like that.'

The temptation was too much for him. 'Dance with me?' he asked.

'Now?' She blinked. 'Hang on. Are you telling me that you can dance like *that*?'

'I worked on an assignment for the medical aid charity with an Argentinean doctor,' he said, 'and she taught us all how to tango. And that dance on the TV just now was much more like a tango than a waltz.'

'Ellis, you always manage to surprise me.' She gave

him a slow, sensual smile that made him catch his breath. 'I'd love to.'

'Go and put some high heels on,' he said, 'and I'll push the furniture back a bit to give us some space.'

'I can't believe you're going to tango with me in my living room.' She was all pink and flustered and absolutely adorable, and Ellis ached to kiss her.

By the time she'd come back, wearing high-heeled shoes, he'd moved the furniture to give them more of a dance floor and connected his iPod to the Internet, to find the music the couple on the television had just danced to. He muted the sound of the television, but he left the picture on.

'Ready?' he asked. At her nod, he said, 'Just follow my lead.'

The music was sexy and intense, like the dance itself, and her eyes were so dark they were practically navy.

Ellis loved every second of having her in his arms, leaning close and making her sway with him in the corners.

At the very end, he bent her backwards over his arm. Her throat was bared to him, and he couldn't resist kissing his way along the arch of her throat.

'That,' he said huskily, 'was what Friday was supposed to be.'

He could see the pulse beating at her throat; the dance had clearly affected her just as much as it had affected him.

'Ellis, I...just, wow,' she said, her voice deeper than usual and slightly breathy. 'I had no idea you could do that.'

'We had someone on the team who could play the

guitar really well. He used to play while Sofia taught the rest of us to dance,' he said.

'It never occurred to me that you'd have time off, time to have fun together. I thought when you worked with a medical aid charity, it was intense and full on.'

'It was, but we still managed to find some good times—even in the middle of a disaster zone,' he said. 'And that helped us get through the rougher times at work. The days when our skills just weren't enough.'

'I can understand that,' she said. 'Ellis, can I be greedy and ask if we can do it again?'

He'd really have to resist the urge to carry her off to her bed afterwards. But he'd find the strength, if it meant pleasing her.

He put the music on again, and exaggerated the moves of the dance so their bodies were closer still, this time. Though he resisted kissing her at the end. There was only so much his self-control could take, and kissing her again would definitely make it snap.

'That,' she said softly, 'was amazing. Thank you.' She smiled. 'You're a bit of a dark horse, Ellis Webster.'

'Maybe. Let's watch the rest of the show,' he said, and settled her back on his lap on the sofa.

When the show finished, he kissed her lightly. 'And now I really do have to go. I'm on early shift tomorrow.'

'Thank you for today, Ellis. I really enjoyed it.' She kissed him back. 'Can we, um, do this again?'

'Date or dance?'

'Both,' she said.

He smiled. 'Let's sort out our off-duty tomorrow. And maybe we should make another list, this time of places we want to go.'

'Top of mine would be Hampton Court Maze,' she

said promptly. 'I've never, ever been there. Considering how long I've lived in London, that's atrocious.'

'Then we'll do that, the next day we both have off,' Ellis said.

'Provided it isn't raining,' she said with a grin. 'I have a feeling that the maze won't be as much fun if we get drenched through.'

'Agreed.' He kissed her again. 'Sleep well. And I'll see you at work tomorrow.'

CHAPTER SEVEN

RUBY LAY CURLED on the sofa with a midwifery journal, not really concentrating on the articles because she was still thinking about Ellis.

She'd had no idea that he could even dance, let alone dance well. He'd really made her pulse speed up when he'd twirled her round and bent her back over his arm like that. And when he'd kissed her throat…She shivered at the memory. Ellis Webster was the first man since Tom who'd made her feel that thrill of attraction, and it threw her.

She turned the page, scanned the headline of the article and did a double-take.

By a strange coincidence, this article might just have a bearing on the court case Ellis was dealing with. She read through the whole thing more carefully and decided that yes, it was definitely relevant and Ellis needed to see this. She went in search of the sticky notes she kept in her kitchen drawer, so she could mark the first page of the article for ease of reference.

The next morning, Ruby caught Ellis during his break. 'Do you have a moment?' she asked.

'Sure. What's the problem?'

'It's a solution, I hope,' she said. 'You know the DNA

tests said that Grace Edwards wasn't the genetic mother of her own baby?'

'Yes.'

'Did you have a word with Theo or the genetics team about it?'

'I haven't managed to get hold of the genetics team, yet,' he said, 'but I did talk to Theo, and he's scratching his head about it as much as I am. Why?'

'Because I might just have a theory. I was reading a midwifery journal last night and there was a case study from America that reminded me of Grace Edwards's situation. I brought it in with me so you could read it. Hang on a sec and I'll get it from my locker.' She fetched the journal and handed it to him. 'I've marked the first page of the article with a sticky note at the top. I might be misreading things, but it also might be that Grace Edwards has the same biological quirk as the woman in the case study—that she's a chimera, so she has two sets of DNA in her body instead of the usual single set.'

Ellis skimmed swiftly through it and raised his eyebrows. 'You know, I think you could be right, Rubes. So maybe Grace started life as a twin, with two separate eggs fertilised by two different sperm. Then, at some point very early in the pregnancy, the eggs fused together and Grace absorbed her twin.'

'So Grace has two sets of DNA and she's also her own twin.'

'Yup.' Ellis blew out a breath. 'Which is pretty mind-blowing.'

'According to that article, having two sets of DNA means that your skin might not have the same DNA as say your heart or your lungs,' Ruby said.

'So it's possible that the cells in Grace's ovaries

originally belonged to her twin and not to her. And in that case it means that her twin is the biological mum of the baby,' Ellis said thoughtfully.

Ruby nodded. 'And that might be why Grace's DNA isn't showing as being the same as that of her baby. It was awful for the poor American mum in the article. She had to have someone appointed by the court to be there at the birth of her next child to witness that she gave birth to the baby. And then, when they did the genetic tests, there was no genetic link between the mum and the baby—even though the court witness was able to say that she definitely gave birth to the baby. Then they did some more tests on cells from different organs in the mum's body, and discovered a match for their DNA.'

'In the case of a chimera, you can't predict which cells will have which twin's DNA. So, as you said earlier, you could have a case where someone has skin and blood cells from one twin and organ cells from another,' Ellis said thoughtfully. 'And the only way to find out is to test several different sorts of cells for DNA to see if they match. Rubes, you're a genius.'

'Hardly,' she said. 'I just happened to see a case study in a journal.'

'But you made the connection,' he pointed out. 'At least now I can give the court a professional opinion, and Theo will back me up so we can suggest they do further DNA tests. Can I borrow this journal for a while?'

'Of course you can.' She smiled at him. 'I'll let you get on.'

'Just a sec. When are you next off duty?'

'Thursday.'

'Me, too. How about going to Hampton Court, if it's not bucketing down with rain?'

'Sounds good to me,' she said.

'It's a date,' he said softly, and Ruby felt warm all over.

Wednesday was a stickier day. As soon as Ruby spoke to the woman who'd come in to the antenatal walk-in clinic, she knew this was a case she really didn't want Ellis to deal with—it was something that would bring back difficult memories for him.

'I just can't keep anything down,' Mrs Bywater said. 'I've read all the books and I've done everything they say I should do about morning sickness. I don't cook anything, I have cold foods rather than hot foods and I stick to super-boring bland things that don't smell.' She grimaced. 'But the problem is, *everything* smells. My mum said I ought to come in and see you because this isn't normal and I've been like this for a month. It's not morning sickness—it's morning, afternoon and night, and I'm losing weight when I'm meant to be putting it on.'

'I think you have something called hyperemesis gravidarum. It's a severe form of morning sickness which affects about one in a hundred women,' Ruby explained. 'It can run in the family. Do you know if your mum ever had it, or do you have a sister who's had it?'

'Just a brother,' Mrs Bywater said. 'I don't think Mum was sick like this when she was pregnant, but I do know she had postnatal depression.' She gave Ruby a wry smile. 'I guess I've got that to look forward to as well.'

'Not necessarily, though we will keep an eye on you

and make sure you get plenty of support.' Ruby poured her patient a glass of cold water. 'Sip this slowly,' she said. 'From the urine sample you gave me, I think you're quite dehydrated and I want to admit you to the ward— we'll need to take blood samples and give you some fluid through a needle into your veins.'

'And then I'll stop being sick?' Mrs Bywater asked.

'You're twelve weeks at the moment,' Ruby said, looking at her notes. 'I hate to tell you this, but often hyperemesis lasts until twenty weeks, and some people find that it lasts a bit longer than that.'

'No.' Mrs Bywater gave a sharp intake of breath. 'I don't think I can cope with that. I just feel so *ill* all the time. And for it to go on for months and months...' She shuddered.

'There are some things you can do,' Ruby said. 'Keep a log of what you eat and when you're ill, so you can see if there's a pattern about timing or types of food that you find difficult. Eating little and often is better than having big meals, and when you do manage to eat something you need to sit upright for a while afterwards, to reduce the likelihood of getting gastric reflux.'

'And don't clean my teeth straight after eating, take lots of small sips of cold water or suck on an ice cube, and try and get as much fresh air as possible,' Mrs Bywater said.

Ruby smiled at her. 'You've definitely been reading up. That's all really good advice. I'm going to admit you, at least for today and maybe tomorrow as well, and we'll give you some fluids to hydrate you and replenish your electrolyte levels. And then you can get some proper rest.'

She'd hoped to catch one of the other obstetricians

when she went up to the ward, but Ellis would have to be the first one she saw.

'I think,' she said carefully, 'maybe you're not the right doctor for this particular mum and I need one of the others instead.'

'Why?' he asked.

She lowered her voice. 'Because this particular mum has hyperemesis.'

Hyperemesis gravidarum. The condition that hadn't been treated properly and had led to his sister's death. 'No. Actually, I'm *exactly* the right person to treat her,' Ellis said firmly. Because then he could make quite sure that what had happened to Sally wouldn't happen to this particular mum.

'Ellis, are you sure you want to do this?' Ruby rested her hand on his arm.

He nodded. 'I know you mean well, and thank you for thinking about me. But I need to do this.'

'If you're sure.' She still wasn't sure about this. At all. Surely treating a patient with this condition would rip open old scars?

'I'm very sure,' he said softly.

And she knew he would be totally professional—he always was. Just at what cost to his heart? Pushing away her misgivings, Ruby took him over to the side room and introduced him to Mrs Bywater. 'Dr Webster's very experienced,' she said, 'and he'll be able to help you.'

'Thank you. I...Excuse me!' Mrs Bywater clapped a hand over her mouth, clearly just about to be sick.

Ruby swiftly handed her a kidney bowl. 'Here. It's fine.'

When Mrs Bywater had finished being sick, Ruby

took the bowl away, first making sure there was a clean one to hand if she needed it.

'Poor you,' Ellis said sympathetically. 'Have a sip of water to make your mouth feel a bit better.'

'Nurse Fisher said I might be like this until twenty weeks—or even later,' Mrs Bywater said miserably.

'Unfortunately she's right, but there are a number of things we can do to help,' he said gently. 'Firstly we need to give you some fluids to hydrate you and re-plenish your electrolyte levels. I'm going to use something called Ringer's solution, because it gives you the extra levels of calcium and potassium. Before we start, though, we're going to check the levels of minerals in your blood so we can make sure we balance everything out for you.'

If the doctor who'd treated Sally had thought to do that before hydrating her, and given her thiamine, she wouldn't have ended up developing the complication of Wernicke's encephalopathy...

Ellis pushed the thought away and concentrated on his patient. 'And you need some rest,' he said. 'I'm guessing that you're not sleeping so well.'

'I'm even sick in the night,' she said. 'And my ribs hurt from being sick all the time. I was even spitting up blood this morning—that's what scared me into com-ing to the walk-in clinic.'

'Being sick puts a bit of strain in the small blood ves-sels of your throat,' Ellis said, 'and it causes them to rupture, so that's why you've seen blood. But it's hon-estly nothing to worry about.' He took the blood sample swiftly. 'We can also give you some medication to help with the sickness.'

Mrs Bywater looked anxious. 'But doesn't that cause problems for baby if I take medication?'

'Anti-sickness drugs did cause developmental issues in babies years and years ago—in the years before you were born,' he said, 'but I'm glad to be able to reassure you that the modern drugs don't affect the baby at all. And the medication will make you feel a lot better— it'll help you to function normally again.'

'All I want to do is feel normal again,' Mrs Bywater said feelingly. 'I don't think I'm ever going to have another baby if pregnancy's always going to make me feel like this!'

'I'm afraid that women who have hyperemesis are more likely to have it in future pregnancies,' he said. 'It just means you'll need to plan ahead to make sure you get the right support and help next time.'

She shook her head. 'There's definitely not going to be a next time. I can't cope with this for a second time.'

'Ruby will finish booking you in,' he said, 'and then as soon as your blood results are back I'll know what to put in the drip. And I promise you, in the next few hours you're going to feel an awful lot better.'

'Thank you,' she said. 'You've been so kind.'

'That's what I'm here for,' he said. 'And if you're worried about anything at all, no matter how little or silly you think the question might be, just ask me or Ruby. Or you can ask any of the team on the ward, because they're all really nice. And we'll make sure you're feeling better as soon as possible.'

Once the blood results were back, Ellis checked the additions to the Ringer's solution with Ruby. 'Given that she's dehydrated, I think we need to warm the area with compresses before we put a needle in, and warm the first litre of fluid so it doesn't come as a shock to her.'

'Good idea,' Ruby said.

He went over to Mrs Bywater and explained what they were going to do.

'Why do you have to put a warm compress on my hand?' she asked.

'It makes your veins dilate a little bit so it's easier for me to put the needle in,' Ruby explained, doing precisely that. 'And it's easier for you, too.'

'Thank you,' Mrs Bywater said.

'That's what we're here for,' Ellis said with a smile. 'I'm going to get you rehydrated, then we'll give you some anti-sickness medication and you can get some well-earned rest.'

After her shift, Ruby headed for Ellis's office where she could see him catching up with paperwork. She rapped lightly on the door. 'Hey.'

He looked up. 'Hey, yourself.'

'I'm taking you for ice cream,' she said.

'Why?'

'Because ice cream always makes things better.'

'I'm fine,' he said.

She put her hands on her hips and stared at him. She knew he wasn't fine. His grey eyes had gone all haunted, and she had a pretty good idea why. Just as she'd suspected, Mrs Bywater's case had brought back all the bad memories for him. He'd helped the patient, but at what cost to himself?

Ellis had been there for her in her darkest days; and she wanted to be there for him, on one of his own dark days.

'OK. You're right,' he admitted at last. 'Give me twenty minutes to finish the paperwork?'

'Fifteen. And no more than that.' She didn't want to give him time to brood. Time to hurt.

He followed her instructions to the letter and they went to a café just round the corner. Ruby bought them both a sundae.

'Was how I felt that obvious?' Ellis asked.

'No, not at all. You were totally professional. I only worked it out because I have privileged information,' she said.

'I guess.' Ellis ate his ice cream in silence, and Ruby let him because she knew it was pointless pushing him until he was ready to talk.

Finally he put his spoon into the cone. 'They thought Sally just had some kind of bug,' he said. 'There had been a virus doing the rounds making people throw up, and she'd had something like it a month or so before. Nobody even considered Sally might be pregnant. She was on the Pill. She took it properly and she wasn't careless; she didn't miss a dose.'

But being sick meant that the medication was less effective, Ruby knew. Maybe Sally hadn't realised that she needed to use extra protection for the next fortnight to make sure she didn't accidentally fall pregnant.

'I don't think anyone out there realised that what she was suffering from was an extreme form of morning sickness.' A muscle twitched in his cheek. 'Unless you've read up on it or you work in the area, you wouldn't know that hyperemesis can start as early as four weeks of pregnancy—maybe even before you realise that you're pregnant. So I get why everyone assumed it was just a bug again.' He blew out a breath.

'They called the medic to see her. He knew she'd been vomiting a lot, so he assumed that she needed rehydrating and gave her IV fluids.' He paused. 'Without checking her thiamine levels first.'

Ruby had a nasty feeling she knew what was coming next, because prolonged vomiting depleted the body's thiamine levels. Rehydration with a solution containing dextrose would deplete the thiamine levels even further, leading to more problems. 'And she developed Wernicke's encephalopathy?' she asked.

He nodded. 'She had visual disturbances and an unsteady gait, and she was disoriented. The classic triad symptoms, in hindsight—but everyone assumed it was just the virus making her throw up all the time that had knocked her for six and made her wobbly on her feet.' He dragged in a breath. 'She ended up with DIC.'

Ruby knew that disseminated intravascular coagulation was where the blood didn't clot properly, and if it wasn't treated the patient could go into shock or even organ failure.

'She went into organ failure,' Ellis continued softly. 'She collapsed and she never regained consciousness.'

'You do know that's not going to happen to *your* patient, don't you?' she asked.

He nodded. 'I've never had any patients out in the field with it, so I haven't lost anyone there.'

She reached out and held his hand. 'So basically when you're working for the aid charity, you're trying to stop what happened to your sister happening to anyone else.'

'That or any other condition.' He paused. 'I guess I know I can't save everyone.'

'Nobody can, no matter how good a medic they are.

Sometimes you just can't save someone, because the circumstances mean that nobody could save them. All you can do is your best, and that has to be good enough because you can't humanly do any more,' Ruby said softly.

'I know.'

Intellectually, maybe, but she could tell he didn't feel it in his heart. 'Obviously I didn't know your sister, but I bet she's looking down on you right now, and I bet she's so proud of the man you've become.'

'I hope so.' He squeezed her hand. 'I didn't mean to go all brooding on you, Rubes. Sorry.'

'Don't apologise. It must be hard when you come across the same condition that took your sister. That's why I didn't want you to see Mrs Bywater.'

'I know, but I'm glad I did—because I feel I've made a difference.'

'Even though it's ripped the top off your scars?' she asked.

He nodded. 'It's harder knowing that if Sally had been given the right treatment she would've survived—but I guess that's true of a lot of my patients. I know I can make a difference. And that's one of the reasons why I love doing what I do. I can stop other families falling apart the way mine has.'

'Tom said your parents closed off afterwards.'

He sighed. 'Now I'm older, I can understand why. They're protecting themselves from more hurt.'

'It must've been hard on you and your brothers, though. Especially as you were so young.'

'They were sixteen and fourteen, and I was twelve.' He lifted a shoulder in a half-shrug. 'We got by. We had each other.'

'I'm glad you're close to them.'

He wrinkled his nose. 'I was. But we fell out a bit after I graduated. They were pretty upset about me working abroad, and they still haven't really got used to it, even after all these years. They think I'm putting myself in danger.'

'That's because you *are* putting yourself in danger—whether you're working in a war zone or in an area hit by flood, earthquake or whatever,' she pointed out.

'I'm still here.' He shrugged it off. 'Anyway, Tom's parents have been like second parents to me. They were brilliant when it all happened.'

'I'm glad—and I'm glad they still have you.'

'And they have you,' he said softly. 'And now, can we please change the subject, Rubes?'

'Sure.' Though Ruby couldn't stop thinking about it for the rest of the evening. The way he'd talked, it sounded as if he wanted to be back at the medical aid charity and he might not want to come back after his assignment. So she'd better be sure not to lose her heart to him completely...

Thursday turned out to be a perfect autumn day, with blue skies and a crispness to the air. Ellis and Ruby caught the train down to Hampton Court.

'What a gorgeous building,' she said as they got their first view of the house.

'Shall we walk round the gardens first, in case the weather changes?'

'Good idea—and I really want to see the maze,' she said.

Funny, as a child, she'd been faintly bored when her parents took her to stately homes, always more keen on spending time in the adventure playground than looking at the plants. Now, she loved strolling through the gardens, enjoying the skill of the designer in highlighting colours and shapes. The autumn colours in the old tilting yard were particularly gorgeous, and she loved the formality of the Privy Gardens with its geometric designs and its statues, and seeing the fountains and the swans on the lake. Walking hand in hand with Ellis, Ruby felt a burst of happiness that had been missing from her life for a long while. And she intended to enjoy every second of it.

'So this is the oldest hedge maze in the world,' she said as she read the information board at the entrance to the maze.

'Apparently it takes twenty minutes to get to the centre.' Ellis smiled at her. 'Are you ready for this?'

'I'm ready,' she said, smiling back.

They took several wrong turns among the yew hedges, and Ellis kissed her in every dead end. Although it took rather longer than twenty minutes to reach the centre, Ruby didn't care; today was all about having fun and enjoying the moment.

'I love all the sound effects they've put in to the maze,' she said. 'When you think you can hear children laughing, or the swish of skirts—it's almost like hearing the ghosts of the past, little glimpses in time of what it might have been like here.'

Ellis looked at her. 'I can just imagine you in Tudor dress. With your colouring, I think you'd have looked fabulous in a rich blue velvet. Like your eyes.'

She stole a kiss. 'Very poetic, Dr Webster. And I can see you in a cloak and a velvet hat. A royal purple one.'

He started to sing 'I'm Henry the Eighth, I am', and she groaned.

'I think I might be creating a monster, here.'

He just laughed. 'Let's go and have a look round the house.'

When they got to the house itself, they discovered that you could actually borrow a red velvet cape.

'I think we ought to do this,' Ruby said with a smile.

'Absolutely,' he agreed.

The rich red velvet suited his colouring, and she could imagine him as a courtier in Tudor times. As tall, as strong and as handsome as the young King Henry VIII himself.

She loved the chapel with its rich blue and gold ceiling, and the tapestried hall where Shakespeare's men had once played. But the bit that really caught her attention was the chocolate kitchen.

'Funny, I always associate Henry VIII with Hampton Court. I never really think about the later kings and queens who lived here,' she said. 'But having a special chocolate kitchen—why on earth would they keep it separate from the other kitchens?'

'This was built for William and Mary,' the guide told them. 'Chocolate was a very expensive drink back then, so it was reserved for the aristocracy. The chocolate maker was one of the highest ranking servants in the palace. He had his own bedroom, which was huge luxury back then, plus he was one of the few people who was actually allowed to serve the king in his private apartments.'

'So was the chocolate they drank very different to what we have today?' Ruby asked.

'They made it all by hand. They roasted the cocoa beans on the fireplace over there—' the guide indicated the area '—and then the kitchen boy took off the shells. They put the cocoa nibs on a heated stone slab and crushed them into a paste with a stone roller, then put the paste into moulds to set into a cake.' He showed them the little cakes of chocolate in cases of waxed paper.

'Was that for eating?' Ellis asked.

'No, bar chocolate wasn't invented until almost Victorian times. The chocolate back then was just for drinking,' the guide explained. 'They'd mix one of these chocolate cakes with water, wine or milk in a pan, then add sugar and spices—the most popular ones were vanilla or chilli. And the king would have hot chocolate for breakfast along with some sweetmeats.' He smiled at them. 'Actually, the palace kitchens have already made the sweetmeats, and we're going to have a demonstration and make drinking chocolate the old-fashioned way for visitors to taste, if you'd like to come back and see us this afternoon. The demonstrations are on the hour, every hour.'

'That sounds great. Thank you,' Ruby said with a smile.

'That's the sort of thing I can imagine you and Tina doing,' Ellis said when they'd moved on to let the guide talk to other visitors. 'Having hot chocolate and sweetmeats for breakfast.'

Ruby laughed. 'I'll have you know that cake for breakfast is one of life's great pleasures.'

'I was right, you are a hedonist,' Ellis teased.

'You bet.' She smiled back at him. 'Life's for living, Ellis.'

'Yes. It is.' His hand tightened round hers.

They continued looking round the house, and went back to the kitchens later in the afternoon for the choc-

olate demonstration. Ruby preferred the vanilla chocolate, but Ellis preferred the chilli.

'A bit like the Spanish explorers who discovered
chocolate,' she said. 'I can see you as one of them. A
Conquistador.'

And that was where Ellis really fitted: not in the city,
but in a wilder place. So it would be wise not to lose
her heart to him, because one day his itchy feet would
take him back to where he belonged. He'd teased her
about being a hedonist; but she'd never been able to
see the attraction of having a holiday in a tent, sleeping on the ground and without running water. In some
respects, they were total opposites and this was never
going to work out.

But for now, she was going to live in the moment and
just enjoy this thing blossoming between them.

On Sunday afternoon, Ruby went shopping with her
best friend. Tina was going to be godmother to her sister's baby and needed a suitable outfit, and Ruby had
promised to go help her find something.

'It's a shame it didn't work out with Roger,' Tina
said, referring to her new colleague.

'He's a nice guy,' Ruby said. 'But I'm not sure he's
ready for dating again yet. I don't think he's over his
divorce, poor man.'

'So what about you? Did you sign up with that online dating agency?'

'Not yet.'

Tina gave her a narrow look. 'Is there something
you're not telling me?'

Yes, Ruby thought, but it was too early to talk about
it. There was definite attraction between her and Ellis,

but would he ever be ready to settle down? She said with a smile, 'Why don't you try this dress on? I think it'll really suit your colouring.'

'You're trying to distract me. So there *is* something,' Tina said. 'OK. You can spill the beans now, or I'll interrogate you over coffee and you can spill the beans then.'

'That's not exactly a choice, Tina.'

'I'm your best friend, Rubes. Who else are you going to tell?'

'True. All right. I'm seeing someone,' Ruby admitted, 'but it's early days.'

'Who?'

'We both want to keep it quiet,' Ruby warned.

Tina flapped a dismissive hand. 'You know perfectly well I'm not going to tell anyone. Who is it, Rubes?'

'Ellis.'

'Ellis? You mean Ellis Webster?' Tina looked surprised.

'What's wrong with Ellis?' Ruby bit her lip. 'Is it because he's Tom's best friend, so it's not appropriate?' It was something that had worried her—how people would react to their relationship.

'No, it's not that.'

'Why, then?'

'It's because Tom always said that Ellis would never settle down—and he's been back in England for a year and a half or so,' Tina said. 'And isn't he planning to go back to the medical aid charity?'

'He's booked to go out with them for a month in a few weeks' time, yes. But that doesn't mean he'll stay out there. If Billie decides to take a career break, then Theo might offer Ellis the job,' Ruby said.

'And is Ellis ready to settle down in England?'

That was something Ruby wasn't sure about. And, if not, would Ellis feel trapped by her? 'I don't know,' she admitted.

'That's what worries me,' Tina said gently, giving her a hug. 'That he still has itchy feet, and you'll lose him to his job and end up hurt.'

'Or we might both decide we're best off just being friends.'

'Maybe.' Tina paused. 'What do you really want, Ruby?'

'To keep seeing Ellis, and for him to settle here. I've felt like this about him for a while,' Ruby admitted. 'I was going to sign up for that dating agency, but I asked him to give me a male point of view on my list of what I wanted in a date. It turned out that he ticked every single one of the boxes.' She paused. 'And I teased him into doing the same—and I ticked all his boxes, too. So we, um, thought we'd give it a try.'

'Then I hope, for both your sakes, that it works out,' Tina said, giving her another hug. 'As long as he makes you happy. But if he ever hurts you...'

'He won't. Not intentionally,' Ruby said.

'Just don't fall for him too hard,' Tina said softly. 'He's a nice guy, but he has itchy feet—and you don't.'

'As I said, it's early days,' Ruby said lightly. 'Now, are you going to try on this dress?'

Tina let her off the hook and went to try on the dress. But it left Ruby wondering. Was Tina right? Should she start backing off from Ellis? Was she hoping for too much? Or was it just way too early even to be thinking about the future and she should just enjoy the moment?

CHAPTER EIGHT

LATER IN THE WEEK, Helen Perkins was scheduled for another intra-uterine blood transfusion for the baby. Ellis made sure that she was booked in with him, and Ruby made sure that she was there to support Helen and Joe.

Ruby had heard nightmare stories from other nursing colleagues about arrogant doctors with non-existent people skills who never listened to the patients because they always thought they knew best, and seemed to forget that they were dealing with people rather than a textbook case. But, apart from the fact that Theo wouldn't let anyone like that work on his ward, since Ruby had been working with Ellis she'd found that he was a natural with patients.

She liked the way he chatted to the Perkinses, and explained what he was doing at each step and answered every question they had without making them feel stupid. And she really liked the way he stayed for a little while after the procedure rather than rushing off to his next patient, making sure that Helen and Joe weren't worried about anything. Dr Ellis Webster was definitely a good man. And she couldn't quite get her head round the fact that they were actually dating. They were still keeping their relationship to themselves, but Ruby was beginning to believe that she'd been granted a second chance at happiness, with a man who could make her as happy as Tom had.

'Next time you come in for the baby's transfusion,' Ellis said to Helen Perkins, 'you'll probably be the one to tell me what happens next.'

'An overnight stay in the ward, and I have to tell you straight away if I have any pain or fever. And I mustn't worry if I can't feel the baby moving for the next couple of hours, because the sedative takes a little time to wear off,' she said with a smile.

He smiled back. 'I stand corrected—I think you're already my star pupil.' He moved the screen so the Perkinses could see the baby's heart beating and be reassured that all was well. 'One snoozing baby,' he said. 'So everything's just as we expected.'

'Thank you, Dr Webster.' Joe Perkins shook his hand. 'We really appreciate this.'

'I know, but it's my job and I don't want any of my new parents to worry,' Ellis told him. 'I'd much rather you asked me a gazillion questions than went away worrying.'

What if I asked you questions? Ruby thought. Would you answer them as honestly as you answer your patients? Or would it scare you away? But she kept her counsel and accompanied the Perkinses up to the ward.

The following Monday morning, Theo called Ellis into his office.

'Billie wants to come back part-time in a month and a half, as a job share,' he said. 'I'm currently arguing budgets with the suits. At the moment, they're saying no, but I'm looking at my figures again to prove that we need another full-time obstetrician on the team and I'm pretty sure I can make a solid case. I know you're going back to the medical aid charity for a month's assignment, but I'm hoping you're planning to come back afterwards and I'd like to interview you for the job.' He smiled. 'It's a formality, really, simply because I have to advertise the position, but I want to offer you the job. Bottom line, Ellis, you're a good fit in the team. You've got the right attitude towards our patients, you've got much wider experience than anyone else at your level, and you're really good at teaching the younger staff and giving them confidence. I'd like you here for good.'

'Thank you,' Ellis said, inclining his head in acknowledgement of the compliments. 'But right now I don't actually know what I'll be doing in a month's time, and it wouldn't be fair to leave you hanging on.' Would the lure of his former job make him want to stay on for another month? Or would he come back to London to be with Ruby? Would it all work out between them? It was still too early to tell—and he didn't want to make the same mistake he'd made with Natalia, rushing into the relationship only to discover that they wanted different things. Yes, he'd known Ruby for an awful lot longer—but until a couple of weeks ago their relationship had been strictly platonic.

Was Ruby the one who'd make him want to settle?

And what if he let her down, the way he felt he'd let Natalia down?

'Think about it,' Theo said. 'Don't say yes or no right now. Think about what you really want.'

'Thank you.'

'For what it's worth, I think you and Ruby are good together.'

Ellis stared at his boss in shock. Theo *knew*?

The question must have been written all over his face, because Theo said softly, 'She hasn't said anything to me, and nobody's gossiping about you. Don't worry, you're not the hot topic on the hospital grapevine.'

'So how on earth do you…?' Ellis was still too flabbergasted to frame the question properly.

Theo smiled. 'Because I've been there myself, when I started dating Maddie. And I definitely needed a good shaking at one point. Just make sure that doesn't happen to you.' His smile faded. 'And if you do decide to accept the job offer and stay here, remember that nothing, but *nothing*, disrupts my team here.'

'Agreed,' Ellis said. 'Patients are always my priority at work. And I'm professional enough to keep my private life very separate from my job.'

'Good.' Theo shook his hand again. 'We'll leave it open for now, but come and see me when you're ready to make a decision. I want you to say yes to the interview, if nothing else. But when I offer you the job—because I really can't see that any other candidate will be better than you—I also want you to be absolutely sure about it, OK?'

'OK.'

Ellis caught Ruby on her break. 'Are you busy after work?'

'Nothing I can't move. Why?'

'I could do with bouncing some ideas off someone.'

'I'm your woman,' she said immediately.

Yes, I rather think you are, he thought. But does that

scare you as much as it scares me? 'Let's do it over dinner. Is tapas OK with you?'

'Tapas would be lovely.' She smiled at him. 'See you after our shift, then.'

After work, Ruby and Ellis went to a small Spanish bar in the middle of London. She settled back in her seat. 'This place is very nice. I haven't been here before,' she said.

'I looked it up online first, and it has good reviews.' He spread his hands. 'Let's just say I learned from that particular mistake.'

'The Date of Disastrous Proportions. Me, too.' She smiled back at him. 'This is a fabulous menu, Ellis. Shall we order a pile of dishes to share?'

'You're welcome to order meat if you want to,' he said. 'You don't have to go vegetarian for my sake.'

'I'm absolutely fine with veggie food. Though I must admit the Serrano ham croquettes do look nice,' she said wistfully, 'if you don't mind me ordering them?'

'No, that's fine.'

They ordered a mixture of dishes—*patatas bravas*, Manchego cheese and quince paste, Manzanilla olives, tomatoes, bread, a bowl of garlicky wilted spinach, the Serrano ham croquettes that had caught Ruby's eye, and a traditional Spanish omelette, together with a bottle of good Rioja.

Ruby had a feeling that Ellis was brooding about something. And it would be better to face it sooner rather than later. 'So what did you want to talk about?' she asked.

'Theo asked me to see him today.' He grimaced.

'Maybe I should shut up now, before I break a confidence.'

'You know I won't say anything to anyone,' Ruby said. 'And it's pretty obvious why Theo would want to talk to you, given that you're Billie's locum and her maternity leave ends soon. So I assume she's coming back?'

'Part-time,' Ellis confirmed.

She bit her lip. 'So where does that leave you?'

'Full-time until she's back. Then I'm doing my month's assignment with the charity.' He paused. 'Theo's looking to recruit another full-time registrar and he wants me to apply for the interview. He says it's a formality but he has to advertise the job externally as well.'

'I get that.' But this was a crunch moment, Ruby thought. Would Ellis apply for the job at the London Victoria, or would he look for a post in a different London hospital—or would he want to stay with the medical aid charity?

Ruby wanted him to stay—but she wanted him to stay because *he* wanted to stay. She didn't want him to feel trapped.

Face it, she told herself. Be brave. Ask him straight out. 'I know you came back to London for Tom's sake, and you've stayed here since he died because he asked you to keep an eye out for me—but what do you really want, Ellis?'

Everything.

Though Ellis was pretty sure he couldn't have Ruby in his life and go back to the medical aid charity. He knew she loved her job here and she was happy in London, so he couldn't ask her to leave it all behind and go travelling the world with him, never staying more than a few weeks in one place.

He really did miss the travelling and the camaraderie of the medical aid charity team, even though he liked his colleagues at the London Victoria very much. There was that extra edge when he worked abroad, where every second was vital.

An old pop song flickered through his head, asking him if he should stay or if he should go.

It was going to be a hard choice. Either way, he was going to have to make a sacrifice. Stay here in London and be with Ruby and miss his old life; or go back to his old life abroad and miss Ruby.

'This thing between us,' he said. 'It's very new.'

'Uh-huh.'

Her face was absolutely expressionless. He had no idea what she was thinking, though he had a feeling that she was trying not to put any pressure on him. Which made him feel horrendously selfish, because Ruby was clearly trying to put him first. He was trying to do the same for her. Were they working at cross-purposes, here? Or could they both have everything they wanted?

The only way to find out was to ask.

'The medical aid charity isn't just for doctors, you know,' he said. 'They recruit nurses, too. Midwives.' He paused. 'If I went back permanently, would you consider going out with me and working for them?'

Her expression changed, then, to one of total surprise. She clearly hadn't expected that to be an option.

Was that a good or a bad thing?

Panicking, he said, 'Ruby, you don't have to answer straight away. I pretty much sprung that on you.'

'Uh-huh.'

And he was all at sea again, not being able to guess how she felt. Though he could see that she looked wary. And he knew it was a huge decision, not one she could make quickly or lightly. 'Take your time,' he said. 'Just think about it in the back of your head, and we'll talk about it again when you're ready.'

'OK.'

He changed the topic of conversation to something light, and when their food arrived they were able to distract themselves with that. Especially when Ruby ordered churros with a cinnamon-spiced chocolate sauce for them to share, and he had to stop himself leaning over and kissing a tiny smear of chocolate from the corner of her mouth.

'I know the coffee here is probably going to be as excellent as the food,' he said, 'but would you like to have coffee back at my place?'

'Good idea,' she said. 'It'll be easier to talk.'

In other words, discussing something in private.

Adrenalin trickled down his spine. Did that mean she'd made a decision about what he'd asked her? Would she go with him, or would she stay?

He paid the bill and they caught the Tube back to his flat. He made them both a coffee and brought out a packet of buttery biscuit curls.

'Now these are nice,' she said with a smile. 'I'm impressed, Dr Webster.'

'Good.' But even the sugar rush couldn't distract him. He needed to know. Now. 'Have you had enough time to think about what I said?' he asked softly.

'Yes.' She took a deep breath. 'I know it's a really worthy thing to do, and I feel horribly selfish about saying this, but working for a medical aid charity really isn't for me, Ellis. I love my job here and I want to stay relatively near to my family and Tom's. Manchester's only a couple of hours away from London on the train, and so is Suffolk. If I work abroad, I won't get to see any of them very often. I might not even be working in a place where I can get a phone signal to talk to them.'

And he knew that Ruby was emotionally close to her family and Tom's. Of course she wouldn't want to be physically far away from them. It was unfair of him to ask her to change that for his sake.

She reached over to squeeze his hand. 'But I also care enough about you to let you go, if you want to go back. I'm never going to hold you back or trap you.'

But it meant he had a choice to make. Go back to working abroad without Ruby: or stay in London and be with Ruby. He couldn't have both.

'What if I apply for the job in our department, come back to London after my assignment and—provided that Theo offers it to me, because he might find a better candidate—I accept the job?' he asked softly. 'Do we take our relationship to the next stage?'

'Is that what you want?'

'To take our relationship to the next stage?' His fingers tightened round hers. 'Yes.'

'But?'

Typical Ruby, picking up what he wasn't saying. 'But the last time I got married, it all went so wrong. And it kind of scares me. If I give up my job abroad, stay here and try to make a go of it with you, and it all goes wrong...' He blew out a breath. 'I don't want to hurt you.'

'I don't want to hurt you, either,' she said. 'So what happened? Why did you split up? I mean—don't get me wrong, I'm not prying, but maybe if you look at what happened you can learn from your mistakes or something?'

'Maybe.' He sighed. 'I met Natalia when we were both working at the medical aid charity. It was one of those *coup de foudre* moments—you know, you meet someone for the very first time and you feel as if you've been struck by lightning. You just click instantly.'

She nodded.

'We were both assigned to a team helping a community after bad flooding. We had a mad affair. And then one day she was caught in a flash flood. Luckily they managed to rescue her. But she could've drowned. She was the first person I've ever been scared of losing—and I guess I acted on that fear instead of thinking it through and letting myself calm down and be logical about things.' He gave her a rueful smile. 'You always say I'm practical and sensible. I wasn't, then. I asked her to marry me, even though we'd barely known each other for a month, and she said yes. And, two weeks later, the paperwork was all sorted and we got married.' He grimaced. 'In a rush. And that's why Tom wasn't my best man. There wasn't enough time to tell him I was getting married and get him a flight out there.' He looked away. 'And I still feel guilty about that. It was supposed to be one of the most special days of my life—the kind of day I'd want my best friend to be part of, too.'

'Just as you were Tom's best man,' she said softly. 'And you flew back to England for three days, so you'd be at our wedding.'

'The year before I got married. Yeah. Which should've told me that I was doing the wrong thing when I married Natalia. I should've talked to Tom about it and at least waited so he could come and be my best man.' He sighed. 'It was a whirlwind romance and we both lost our heads a bit. We didn't really know each other well enough, and we should've waited a while and got to know each other an awful lot better.' He gave her a rueful smile. 'I assumed Natalia loved the job as much as I did and she'd be happy to keep travelling with me, working in a different country every few weeks and seeing the world and knowing we were making a difference. But she wanted something else.'

'Something you didn't?'

He nodded. 'She assumed that getting married meant I wanted to go back to one of our home countries and settle down. Probably a capital city. Moscow or London—she didn't mind which.'

'But you obviously didn't want to settle.'

'No.'

'And you didn't talk any of this through before you got married?'

She sounded surprised—shocked, even. And she had a point. They hadn't thought it through or talked it through. 'I was twenty-five and I still had an awful lot of growing up to do. I guess, so did she. We ended it reasonably amicably, or as amicably as you can end any marriage,' he added. 'We both realised that we shouldn't have got married in the first place; we should have left our relationship as a mad affair and waited for the right person. We lost touch after the divorce, so I have no idea if she found her Mr Right—but I hope she did. I'd like to think she's happy now.'

'Fair enough.'

Ruby's voice was even, but Ellis noticed that she'd gently wriggled her fingers out of his grasp. Did that mean she'd changed her mind about him—that she felt his track record meant that he wouldn't be a good bet for her?

'So do you know what you want out of life now?' she asked. 'Do you still want to go back to the medical aid charity?'

'Yes, I do, because I love my job,' he admitted. 'But part of me wants to stay with you.' Even though the two things were mutually exclusive. Job or Ruby. That was the choice.

'I've already lost someone I loved deeply,' she said. 'I'm not sure I'm ready to take that risk again. I don't want to lose you to your job. So maybe you and I should go back to being just good friends.'

'Is that what you want?' he asked.

'Yes and no,' she said. 'I want to be with you, Ellis. But I also know you need to follow your heart and I'd never stop you doing that. If you decide to stay here in London when you still have itchy feet, then at some point in the future you're going to feel trapped and you'll start to resent me for holding you back. The whole thing's going to end up—' she grimaced '—and please don't think I'm being bitchy, because I'm just trying to be realistic here. I worry that things between us are going to end up like your marriage did. They'll go wrong, because we want different things from life and we haven't talked it through properly. We haven't given each other enough time.'

'I married Natalia in a rush because I was scared of losing her, and I ended up hurting her because it turned out that we didn't want the same things. I've grown up a lot since then,' Ellis said. 'But I admit that over the past few years I've kept my relationships just for fun, so we all know the score and nobody gets hurt.'

'I can understand that,' she said.

'Since I've met you, it's been different,' he said. 'I know Tom loved you deeply, and you loved him. And while Tom was alive I would never, ever have made a move on you. But somewhere over the last eighteen months my feelings towards you changed. I don't think of you as just a friend, Rubes.'

'So what are you saying, Ellis?'

He took a deep breath. Crunch time. 'I want to be with you.'

'We've known each other for a long time, but it's still very early days with us dating. Supposing we find out we really don't want the same things?' she asked.

'Then we'll talk about it and find a way to compromise. Isn't that what a grown-up relationship's meant to be about?'

'I guess so.' She looked at him. 'And that's what you want? A grown-up relationship? With me?'

'I do,' he said softly. 'Right now, I can't promise you that everything's going to work out. That it's all going to be perfect and plain sailing.'

'Nobody can ever promise that,' Ruby said. 'Because life happens and changes things.'

'But what I can promise,' he said, 'is that I'll always try to be honest with you.'

'That's all I can ask for,' she said. 'And it's enough for me.'

'So, you and me.' He took her hand again, and drew it up to his mouth. 'I can't quite believe this is happening.'

'Me, neither.'

'Ruby.' He leaned towards her and touched his lips

to hers. For a moment she remained tense, and then she gave a small sigh and relaxed into his arms.

This was what he wanted.

Ruby, soft and warm and in his arms. Kissing him until they were both dizzy.

He deepened the kiss, and the next thing he knew he was lying on the sofa, with Ruby sprawled on top of him. His hands had slid underneath the hem of her top and were splayed against her back.

'Sorry. I'm taking this a bit too fast,' he said softly, restoring order to her clothes and then sitting up again, moving her so that she was sitting on his lap with his arms wrapped round her.

'Sorry.' She stroked his face. 'And here we are. Apologising to each other and being super-polite.'

'I've wanted you for a long time,' he said. 'But, as you said, this is still early days. I'm happy to wait until you're ready for the next step.'

'Thank you. Because I want this, too—but...'

'I know. It's scary.' He dropped a kiss on her forehead. 'Can I be honest with you? I really don't want our first time together to be in London. I want it to be somewhere else, where neither of us has any memories.'

'Is it going to be a problem? The past, I mean?'

'No.' He was definite about that. 'I'm not trying to compete with Tom, and I know you're not comparing me to him because we're very different men. And I loved Tom dearly—as much as if he was one of my brothers. But I want something that's just going to be for us,' he said. 'I assume you've already been to Paris and Rome with Tom?'

She nodded. 'They're my two favourite cities,' she

said. 'And Tom and I visited a lot of Italy over the years. Florence, Venice, Sorrento, Verona, the Lakes.'

'Not Italy, then. Or Paris. But somewhere just as magical.'

'How about you?' she asked. 'Where's the most magical place you've ever been?'

'The Australian Outback,' he said without hesitation. 'Uluru—Ayers Rock is amazing, Rubes. It glows red at dawn, and purple and blue at sunset. I've never seen anything like it. And the stars are stunning, because there's no artificial light source. You just look up and see the Milky Way and the Magellanic clouds stretching across the sky. It's one of the most incredible sights I've ever seen.'

'Were you there for long?'

'A few days. I wasn't working—I just took the opportunity to get on a plane and spend a couple of weeks travelling round Australia. I was privileged to go on a tour round Uluru with one of the Anangu people. He showed me the springs, caves and rock paintings, and he told me about the Aboriginal dreamtime stories of the area. And we talked about medicine—did you know they use the sap of the centralian bloodwood as a disinfectant and an inhalant for coughs and colds?'

She smiled. 'I should've guessed you'd end up talking about that sort of thing. You're all about the wild and untameable, aren't you?'

'Only in part. I'm guessing that you prefer cities?'

'Ones with pretty buildings, lots of history and good food. I'm not so fussed about shopping,' she said.

'Maybe we could go somewhere together,' he said. 'Just the two of us.'

Her eyes widened. 'And then we take the next step?'

'Not necessarily. No expectations—the same as going out for dinner with you didn't mean that I expected you to go to bed with me. We just spend a bit of time together and take life as it comes. We'll have separate rooms so there's no pressure. If it happens, then fantastic; if it doesn't, then we'll wait until we're both ready.'

'No pressure,' she repeated.

'Is your passport current?'

'Yes.' She stroked his face. 'Are you thinking of soon?'

'Yup. When's your next off-duty where you have three days off in a row?'

'I'll need to check on my phone. Then maybe we can synchronise it.'

'Sure.' He kissed her lightly. 'And we'll see what happens.'

A few days away together, in a place that had no memories for either of them. A place where they'd make new memories. Where maybe they'd make love for the first time.

Part of Ruby was thrilled. She loved the idea of spending time with Ellis, sharing a new city with him, discovering little cafés and art galleries.

Part of her felt guilty. It still wasn't *that* long since Tom's death. Was this too soon?

And part of her wondered if this was the beginning of the end of her relationship with Ellis. She'd seen the wonder in his face when he'd been talking about the Australian Outback, the longing in his eyes when he'd mentioned the medical aid charity. Would the odd few days in Europe really be enough to keep his itchy feet happy? Or would the lure of his job be too much for him, once he went back for that planned month's assignment?

CHAPTER NINE

TRAVELLING AGAIN. EVEN though it wasn't quite the same—he was going simply to have fun, rather than working to make a difference in the world—the idea of seeing another part of the world filled Ellis with joy. Especially because he was going to share it with Ruby. Somewhere new for both of them.

During his lunch break, he went to the travel agent's to pick up some brochures for city breaks, then left Ruby a text.

Have pile of brochures. Want to come and plan our trip after work?

Sorry, can't. On lates until Friday, then I'm going to Manchester for the day to see my family, was her reply.

He damped down the disappointment.

Sure. Let me know when you're free and we'll do it then.

You could come to Manchester with me, if you like?

As her official date?

He wasn't sure he was ready to go public with their

relationship, yet, let alone go to meet her family as her date. Not until they were both sure about where this was going. He knew how he felt about Ruby, but he also knew that he didn't have a good track record. Until he could be absolutely sure that this was going to work out and he wasn't going to hurt her, the way he'd hurt Natalia, he didn't want to make things too official.

Ellis had met Ruby's family at the wedding and at Tom's funeral, and Tom himself had always spoken highly of his in-laws. But meeting them as Tom's best friend was a very different kettle of fish from meeting them as Ruby's partner.

Sorry, working Friday, he typed back. Maybe next time you go?

Ellis and Ruby were both free on Sunday, and spent the afternoon poring over the travel brochures.

'An ice hotel—that sounds really romantic,' Ruby said. 'And we might get to see the Northern Lights. I'd love that.' Her smile faded. 'That was on Tom's bucket list, too. Except we didn't have the time.'

He hugged her. 'I know. Maybe we'll do that another time,' he said softly. 'This is only a short break, and there's no guarantee we'll actually see the lights.'

'Plus the short daylight hours mean we won't have time to explore any of the cities,' she agreed. 'OK. How about Barcelona?'

'Apparently the Sagrada Familia is amazing. So that's a possibility.' He paused. 'Or maybe Vienna.'

'Sachertorte and Mozart,' she said promptly. 'And it'll be late October when we go, so the Austrian Christmas markets might have started, too. That'd be nice.'

'Or,' he said, 'what about the city of a thousand spires?'

'Where's that?'

'Prague. In the Czech Republic. Next door to Austria.'

She grinned. 'That's where you really want to go, isn't it?'

Yes. He'd seen the pictures in the brochures and known immediately that he wanted to visit the city. But how did she know? 'What makes you say that?' he asked carefully.

'The way your eyes lit up when you said it. Like they did when you talked about the stars in the Australian Outback.'

'Busted,' he admitted. 'I, um, sort of made a list. In my head. Nothing formal, and I wouldn't have made a proper list without you.'

She laughed. 'I didn't think you'd be able to wait.'

He hadn't. The itch to travel, and to plan a trip, had been too strong. He *missed* travelling, seeing new places and meeting new people and learning new things.

She glanced through the brochure. 'All those bridges across the river—Prague's very pretty. It reminds me a bit of Florence, or maybe Paris.'

'And at this time of year there might be a chance of a sprinkle of snow. It could be really romantic.'

'Sold. Let's do it,' she said.

'Great. The hotels all seem to be gorgeous art deco buildings.'

'That's lovely. And, by the way, we're going halves on this trip,' she reminded him.

He sighed. 'We've already had this conversation. You know, about accepting gracefully when it's made clear that there are no strings? I just want to spoil you a bit, Rubes.'

'Buying me dinner isn't the same as taking me away for a three-day break, Ellis.'

'I wouldn't offer if I couldn't afford it,' he said softly.

'We're going halves.' She folded her arms.

'How about I pay for the hotel and flights, and you pay for dinner?' he suggested.

'And entrance fees to wherever we go,' she added.

If it made her feel more comfortable, then he'd agree. 'OK.'

'Good.'

Though her arms were still folded and there was a little pleat in her brow—something he'd noticed when she was unhappy about something. 'I'll try and find us somewhere central,' he said. 'And remember I said I'll book separate rooms, so there are no expectations and there's no pressure. We're just going away and enjoying ourselves, exploring somewhere new to both of us.'

To his relief, the frown faded. 'Thank you, Ellis,' she said softly. 'I appreciate it.'

'I know.' He kissed her lightly. 'And we need a guide book.'

She laughed, and he frowned. 'What's so funny?'

'Given that you're such a seasoned traveller, I expected you to—well, just go with the flow.'

'No. When I get the chance to explore somewhere new, I read up about the place in advance so I can plan what I want to see and make the most of my time there.' He smiled. 'I don't do it quite down to the microsecond, but some places are closed on certain days and it'd be a shame to miss out on them because we hadn't bothered to check up beforehand.'

'OK. I'll pick up a guide book tomorrow lunchtime,'

she said. 'I haven't been away for quite a while, so this is really exciting.'

'What I'm most looking forward to,' he said, 'is spending time with you, chilling out and discovering things together.'

'Sounds good to me. So I take it I need to pack walking shoes and comfortable clothes?'

'And maybe a posh dress, in case we decide to have dinner somewhere fancy.'

She laughed. 'Promise you're not going to spill wine all over me?'

He laughed back, knowing she was referring to their disastrous 'first date'. 'I'll try not to.'

Ellis called for Ruby the day of their departure; then they took the train to the airport and queued up at the flight desk to process their baggage.

'So whereabouts is our hotel?' she asked.

'We're just off Wenceslaus Square,' he said, 'so we're about a ten-minute walk from the Old Town Square, and maybe another five minutes from there to the river.'

'That sounds perfect. Thank you.' She stood on tiptoe and kissed him, and it made him feel warm all the way through.

Once they were through customs and passport control in Prague, they saw a taxi driver waiting by the barriers holding a board with the name 'Webster' written on it in capitals,

'I booked the taxi transfer in advance, to save us having to queue,' he explained.

'Which is why your name's on the board.' She smiled. 'I thought that sort of thing only happened in films.'

'Me, too.' He took her hand. 'But it's fun.'

The taxi driver didn't speak English. 'Thanks to working with doctors of all nationalities with the medical aid charity, I've got a smattering of a lot of languages,' Ellis said. 'Though I don't know much Czech beyond please, thank you, hello, goodbye and ordering a couple of beers.'

'Just as well we have a phrase book, then,' Ruby said, taking it from her bag.

The airport was in the middle of the countryside, and they enjoyed the autumnal views on the way to the city. Prague itself was beautiful, with lots of white four- and five-storey buildings with orange roofs. Everywhere they looked, they could see domes, mosaics and lots of windows.

'This is gorgeous. It reminds me a bit of Paris,' Ruby said.

'Me, too—but look.' He gestured to the skyline; there were lots of turrets and towers with spires, all very gothic and very pretty.

'I can see why they call it the city of a thousand spires. There must be a dozen on that tower over there alone.' She smiled at him. 'I'm so looking forward to this, Ellis.'

His fingers tightened round hers. 'So am I,' he said softly.

The taxi drew up outside their hotel. Ellis helped Ruby out of the back of the cab, then tipped the driver. A doorman wearing a top hat took their luggage, and they checked in at the front desk. The hotel reception was gorgeous, all marble and art deco glass; there was a table in the centre containing huge vases with stunning arrangements of lilies and peonies.

'This is amazing,' she said once they'd got their card

keys for their rooms and were heading up in the lift. 'But, Ellis, this must have cost a fortune. It has to be the swishest hotel in Prague.'

'No, the swishest hotel is overlooking the river, actually. I did ask, but sadly their presidential suite is currently booked by a film star,' he said, and laughed. 'Plus it was ever so slightly out of my budget. This isn't.'

'I wasn't expecting this to be so—well...' She gestured round them. 'It's gorgeous, but I feel bad that you've spent so much money on me.'

'Remember what I said about being gracious. I want to do something nice for you, so let me have the pleasure of making you smile.'

'I guess.' She bit her lip. 'Sorry. Now I'm being an ungrateful brat. I didn't mean it like that.'

'I know. But there really are no strings attached. This is just a couple of days for us to explore somewhere new and have some fun,' he said. 'No timetables and no schedules—though I admit I've reserved us a table here tomorrow night, because they have a band playing and I thought it might be fun to dance together after dinner.'

'That sounds lovely.'

'Let's unpack,' he said, 'and then we can go exploring. How long do you need?'

'Ten minutes,' she said.

'Great.' He smiled at her. 'See you out here in ten.'

The room was amazingly swanky. The bed was incredibly wide and very comfortable, and the bathroom was all gleaming marble and thick fluffy towels. It didn't take Ruby long to unpack, and she was ready to meet Ellis in the ten minutes she'd promised.

'I feel thoroughly spoiled,' Ruby said when she

walked through her door to find him waiting in the corridor.

'Good. That was the idea.'

His grey eyes were sparkling with what she guessed was happiness; the same feeling that was bubbling through her.

He smiled and took her hand. 'Let's go and see the sights.'

The city was beautiful and Ruby really enjoyed walking through the Old Town. There were lots of gorgeous art deco buildings with yellow, pink or white walls, a dome on the roof and huge arched windows.

A crowd of people was waiting outside one particular building.

'That's the astronomical clock,' Ellis said when he'd consulted his guide book. 'It's the oldest working astronomical clock in the world, and it shows the movement of the sun and moon through the zodiac.'

'It's so pretty with all those swirling greens and blues and golds.' She glanced at her watch. 'Does something happen on the hour?'

'Apparently the figures move. Shall we wait and see?'

On the hour, the figure of Death struck the bell, to the cheers of the waiting tourists.

'It's amazing that it's six hundred years old and still working,' she said. 'I'm so glad we came here.'

They walked from the old town square down to the Vltava river, then found a small café overlooking the wide, fast-flowing river where they could grab a sandwich and coffee for lunch.

'Would you like to go on a river trip?' Ellis asked.

'That's a great idea. I hardly ever got to go on a boat

as Tom used to get horribly seasick. Even with travel sickness pills, he couldn't handle a gentle cruise down the Thames.'

'I remember,' Ellis said. 'There was a school trip in the South of France where we were supposed to go out in a glass-bottomed boat and see all these amazing fish, except when we got out of the harbour the water was a bit choppy. I didn't get to see any of the fish either, because I was too busy trying to find extra sick bags for him—the crew hadn't brought enough and suggested that people shared bags, and that made Tom throw up even more!'

'Poor Tom. It must have been awful for him—and not that nice for everyone round him, either.' She smiled at him. 'I'm so glad we can talk about him, Ellis. That it's not going to make things awkward between us.'

'We both loved him,' Ellis said simply, 'so it's an extra bond between us. Of course it's not going to be awkward. And I'd never cut him out of my life and refuse to talk about him.' He knew she was well aware of what he hadn't said: the way his parents were about Sally. 'I want to remember the good times and smile about them. Just as I do about Sally.' And how he wished he could fix it for his parents, so they'd still have some of the joy left in their lives. He slid his arm round Ruby's shoulders and gave her a hug.

He held her hand all the way on the river trip. And his fingers tightened round hers when they passed the lover's bridge festooned with padlocks. 'It seems to be a tradition in a lot of European cities now,' she said, 'to put a padlock on a bridge with your initials on it.'

'Which is a bit more environmentally friendly than carving it into a tree trunk,' Ellis said.

Once they were back on dry land, they walked over the Charles Bridge, admiring the statues and the views of the other bridges across the Vltava. 'I can hardly believe this bridge is nearly seven hundred years old,' she said. 'I loved the story the guide on the boat told us about mixing the mortar with eggs to make it stronger. I wonder if that really happened?'

'Who knows? As you say, it was a good story.'

They wandered hand in hand through the streets. Ruby hadn't felt this relaxed in a long time, and she was really enjoying exploring the city with Ellis, stopping whenever something caught their eye to consult the guide book for more information.

They found a small, romantic restaurant serving local dishes, and the waiter smiled in approval when Ellis spoke Czech to order two beers.

'What do you recommend that's typically Czech?' she asked the waiter.

'*Svíčková na smetaně*,' he said, which turned out to be dumplings and beef in creamy sauce with cranberry compote and sweetened whipped cream.

The vegetarian option was *smažený sýr*—a thick slice of cheese, breadcrumbed and fried, served with potato salad.

'It all looks amazing but not so good for our arteries,' she said when the waiter had gone again.

'I'm pretty sure we'll walk it off tomorrow,' he said with a smile. 'I thought we could go and explore the castle.'

'Sounds great,' she said.

The food was excellent; the dumpling was larger than Ruby expected, made into a large roll and sliced. She liked the tartness of the cranberry as it cut through the richness of the cream. 'I definitely need to join you in walking this off tomorrow,' she said with a smile.

Once they'd shared a pudding—a potato dumpling stuffed with plums, steamed, and served with melted butter and a sprinkle of sugar—they walked back to the hotel, enjoying the way the city was lit up at night.

'This was a brilliant idea,' she said. 'Thank you, Ellis.'

'My pleasure.' He slid his arm round her shoulder, and she slid hers round his waist, enjoying his nearness.

Back at the hotel, they ordered hot chocolate at the bar; then finally they headed to their rooms.

Was this when it was going to happen? Ruby wondered, her pulse hammering.

Ellis kissed her goodnight at the door, his mouth warm and sweet and coaxing.

But then he pulled back. 'Goodnight, Ruby. Sleep well.'

Clearly he wasn't expecting her to invite him in to her room—and he hadn't invited her to his, either. So he'd meant it when he'd said there were no strings, no expectations. Odd how that made her stomach give a little swoop of disappointment.

But maybe he was right. Rushing into anything could be a mistake. And he'd admitted to making a huge mistake, rushing in to marriage in the past. He must feel just as wary as she did.

'You, too,' she said brightly, and let herself into her room.

Once she'd showered and cleaned her teeth, she changed into her pyjamas and climbed into bed. She lay there awake, thinking of Ellis. Wandering round such a romantic city with him, hand in hand; the way he'd kissed her at unexpected moments; and the warmth and sweetness of his arms round her.

What would happen if she picked up the phone and dialled his extension?

She thought about it to the point where she actually picked up the phone and dialled the first digit of his room number. But then she replaced the receiver, not wanting to get this wrong and make things awkward between them.

Tomorrow was another day.

Maybe tomorrow.

Ellis lay awake, thinking of Ruby. Outside her door, she'd looked so vulnerable for a moment that he'd wanted to hold her and not let her go. Yet at the same time he hadn't wanted her to feel pressured. He'd booked separate rooms on purpose, to make it clear that he was happy to wait until she was ready to take their relationship to the next step.

What if he called her now?

What if he asked her to come to his room—just to cuddle up and go to sleep together?

But that would be unfair. He didn't want her to feel obliged, just because he'd paid for the trip. Plus it was still early days between them.

He'd wait until she was ready, just as he'd promised himself. He'd keep cool, calm and collected.

But, oh, he wished...

CHAPTER TEN

RUBY HAD BREAKFAST with Ellis the next morning in the hotel restaurant: a mushroom and cheese omelette cooked by the chef, toast, fruit with yoghurt, and freshly squeezed orange juice followed by a cappuccino.

'This is the perfect start to the day,' she said with a smile. 'And it's nice not to be grabbing a granola bar and a banana and eating them on the way to work.'

'So you like being waited on?' Ellis asked.

She laughed. 'No. I'm just enjoying being spoiled. Weren't those your orders?'

'Absolutely.' He smiled back.

It was another crisp, bright autumn day: perfect for exploring. They bought tickets from a kiosk; using a mixture of guidebook Czech and sign language, they found out where the tram stop was and took a tram to the castle. There was a jolt when the tram turned one corner and she stumbled, not quite sure where to grab on to as there weren't overhead bars or straps like there were on the Tube in London. Ellis caught her before she fell.

'Thank you.'

'No worries.'

It felt natural then to wrap her arms round his waist

and stay where she was until they reached the tram stop for the castle.

They had a beautiful view from the hill.

'According to the guide book, this is the largest castle in the world,' he told her.

Ruby could believe it; there seemed to be courtyard after courtyard, and the walls seemed to stretch out for ever.

They went into the oldest section of the castle and walked up a set of wide, shallow brick stairs. 'I have to say, I was expecting narrow stone spiral stairs,' she said, 'like the ones you get in a lot of English castles.'

He consulted the guide book and raised an eyebrow. 'That's because these weren't for people.'

'Not for people? Who were they for, then?' she asked, puzzled.

His eyes sparkled. 'Would you believe, horses?'

'No way!'

'They used to joust in the Vladislav hall, so the knights would ride up these stairs,' he said. 'Honestly. I'm not teasing.'

When they walked into the hall, she realised that he was telling the truth. It was a massive room, very long, with vaulted ceilings, the most enormous windows and huge wrought iron chandeliers. 'I can imagine it. There's enough room for the knights to joust and people to watch them.'

Afterwards, they strolled through the palace gardens, enjoying the amazing view of the city from the castle walls.

'The cathedral reminds me very much of Notre Dame, with the twin towers and the rose window,' she said as they went into yet another courtyard and discovered the cathedral of St Vitus. Inside, she loved the soaring vaulted ceilings and the Mucha window.

'And there's a bell tower... I know they don't have a grotesque gallery here like they do at Notre Dame, but I still think we have to climb it,' Ellis said.

'Agreed,' she said with a smile.

'You look all pink and adorable,' he said when they got to the top.

'You mean, I'm not as fit as I like to think I am,' she said wryly. 'Especially as you're not even glowing, let alone hot and sweaty like I am!'

'Nope, you're all pink and adorable,' he repeated, and kissed her.

They stood looking out at the views, with Ellis standing behind Ruby, his arms wrapped round her and holding her close. Funny how being with Ellis made her feel like a teenager again.

Almost as if he'd picked up on her thoughts, he asked, 'Can I take a selfie?'

'Sure, as long as you send it to me as well.'

He stooped to press his cheek against hers and took a picture of them both smiling. 'Me and my girl,' he said softly, 'and there's the spire to prove we're right at the top of the cathedral.'

Me and my girl. It sent a thrill all the way through her.

They enjoyed wandering through the rest of the castle, visiting the tiny houses in Golden Lane. Ruby was fascinated by the herbalist's house, with its narrow wooden shelves full of stone jars and bottles, with bunches of herbs hanging up to dry from the rafters. 'This is what we would have worked with, all these years ago,' she said.

'In some of the places where I've worked, it's more than we'd have now,' he said. 'Even hot water can be a luxury.'

Ruby wondered again, would Ellis stay with the medical aid charity? Was visiting a place like this enough to stop his itchy feet returning, or was it making things worse? She didn't like to ask him outright—it felt like an ungrateful question, especially as he'd gone to the trouble to make this break special for her—but she remembered Tina's warning. She'd be a fool to let herself fall for someone who didn't want to stay around.

When they'd finished looking round the castle, they grabbed a *trdelník* from one of the fast-food stands just outside the castle gates. The rolled dough was made into a spiral, grilled on a stick and sprinkled with sugar and cinnamon. 'This is gorgeous,' she said after the first taste. 'It's like a cross between the crêpes in Paris and the doughnuts you'd have at the seaside in England.'

They walked through the cobbled streets of the Lesser Quarter into Petrin Park. 'We have to see the Observation Tower while we're here,' Ellis said. 'It's a copy of the Eiffel Tower but about a quarter of the size—though, because it's on a hill, it's actually higher than the Eiffel Tower and the views are meant to be amazing.'

The day had turned windy and when they got to the top of the tower Ruby was a bit taken aback to discover that it actually swayed in the wind. As if Ellis realised what was making her nervous, he wrapped his arms round her again, making her feel safe. 'The guide book was right. The views are amazing,' she said, 'and I think that golden roof is the theatre we passed when we were on the river.'

'And the Dancing House,' he said, pointing out the modern building that looked just like a couple doing the waltz on the other side of the river. 'Maybe we can have a closer look at that tomorrow.'

'Sounds good to me.'

Hand in hand, they walked back to the hotel.

'Our table will be ready in an hour and a half,' he said in the corridor outside their doors. 'Unless that's not giving you enough time to get ready, we could go to the bar for a drink first?' he suggested.

She smiled. 'You know I'm not one of these women who needs hours and hours to do her hair and make-up. A drink at the bar sounds good. Shall I knock on your door when I'm ready?'

'That'd be perfect,' he said with a smile, and kissed her. 'I've really enjoyed today. I'm glad I shared it with you.'

'Me, too—even though that tower was a bit scary when it started swaying,' she said.

Ruby showered, did her hair, changed into the new little black dress she'd bought especially for Prague, and did her make-up. And she felt ridiculously nervous as she knocked on his door.

Ellis was wearing a formal dinner suit and bow tie. She was used to him wearing a suit at work, but this took it to another level. 'You look amazing,' she said, feeling her eyes widen.

'So do you.' He drew her into his arms. 'Right now I really want to kiss you, but I guess I shouldn't smudge your lipstick.'

'You can kiss me later,' she said.

'I hope that's a promise.'

'It is—and I always keep my promises,' she said.

They had a glass of wine in the bar, and then it was time to go into the restaurant. Ruby glanced at the menu and gasped. 'Ellis, it's Michelin-starred.'

'I know, and it counts as part of the hotel bill.'

'It most certainly does not. Our deal was that I'm paying for dinner.'

'You can buy me lunch tomorrow,' he said. 'I'm paying, and you're not allowed to argue. Remember, graciousness.'

She rolled her eyes. 'Thank you. But you really didn't have to.'

Once their waiter had poured the champagne, he brought them both an *amuse-bouche* of ravioli filled with mushrooms and truffles, served with foamed butter.

'This is to die for,' Ruby said.

Ellis smiled. 'What was that in the ad you wrote for me about finding a foodie as a partner?'

She laughed. 'Absolutely.'

The starter was a soft buffalo mozzarella served with rocket and tomatoes and balsamic, light and quivery and beautifully presented. Ellis had beetroot ravioli filled with ricotta and thyme and served with more of the foamed butter, while Ruby had grilled sea bass with Mediterranean vegetables. But the best bit for her was the pudding—crème brûlée, her favourite, and the waiter actually brought a blow-torch to the table along with the dessert. 'There's a tiny drop of brandy on the top so the sugar will be flambéed,' he explained, then set fire to the sugar so it would melt into a hard crust.

'This has to be the best meal I've ever eaten in my entire life,' Ruby sighed when they'd finished.

'From a foodie like you, that's quite a compliment,' Ellis said.

After dinner, as Ellis had promised, there was dancing. A woman with a smoky voice was singing soft jazz, accompanied by a piano, double-bass, and guitar. The lighting was soft and, together with the music, made the room feel very intimate. Ellis swayed with her, holding her close, and Ruby felt as if she could dance all night.

She closed her eyes and gave herself up to the music and his nearness. Right at that moment, she could believe that the two of them were the only ones in the room. And Ellis was an excellent dancer; he led her round the floor so she didn't have to worry about putting a foot wrong.

Finally the singer said goodnight and the band left the stage.

'Do you want to go to back to the bar?' Ellis asked.

'No, I think I've had quite enough alcohol for tonight,' she said. What she really wanted was to ask him to come back to her room with her, but she didn't quite have the nerve to say so; shyness kept the words inside.

'I'll see you back to your room,' he said.

The lift was all mirrors inside, and their reflections stretched out to infinity.

'I could kiss you to infinity right now.' His voice was low and husky, and the words sent a thrill right through her.

'Do it,' she whispered back.

He gave her the sexiest smile she'd ever seen, dipped his head and brushed his mouth against hers. Every nerve-end tingled; she wrapped her arms round him and kissed him back until she couldn't think straight.

There was a soft ding and the lift doors opened.

He broke the kiss, looking dazed.

Somehow they managed to walk out of the lift and down the corridor to their rooms.

He paused outside her door. 'I guess this is goodnight,' he said softly.

She could do the sensible thing and say goodnight.

Or she could give in to the demands flooding her body and ask him to stay.

For a heartbeat she was torn between the two. She knew that making love with Ellis would change things between them again, and supposing it changed things the wrong way?

But she'd never been a coward. If things between them went wrong in the future, then they went wrong. Right here, right now, she knew what she wanted. Ellis.

'What if I don't want it to be goodnight?' she asked, her voice equally soft.

'Are you saying…?'

'Stay with me, Ellis.'

'Are you sure about that?'

'Very sure.' She took her card key from her evening bag, slipped it into the lock and opened her door.

Then he scooped her up in his arms and carried her into the room. He nudged the door closed behind them, then set her back on her feet, keeping her body close to his so she was left in no doubt about how much he wanted her.

The curtains were already closed, and there was just the low light of the bedside lamp.

'It feels as if we should have candlelight,' he said.

'This is the next best thing,' she said. 'It'd probably set the fire alarms off if we had candles in here anyway.'

'You're so practical. It's one of the things I love about you.'

'Thank you.' She inclined her head in acknowledgement of the compliment.

'Something else I love,' he said, 'is your mouth.' He traced the curve of her lower lip with the tip of his finger. 'It's a perfect cupid's bow.'

She opened her mouth and drew the tip of his finger inside, then sucked hard.

He gasped and his eyes darkened. 'Ruby, you drive me crazy. I want you so much. I've wanted you for so long.'

'I want you, too.' She reached up and undid his bow tie.

He smiled at her. 'Oh, so this is the way we're doing it, is it?' He spun her round, unzipped her dress, then kissed a path all the way from the nape of her neck to the base of her spine, sliding the dress down her body as he did so.

She stepped out of the dress and turned to face him. 'My turn.' She started undoing the buttons of his shirt. Her fingers were a little clumsy, but it didn't matter; the heat in his expression encouraged her to keep going. He shrugged off his jacket, and she untucked his shirt from his trousers so she could finish undoing it and slide the soft cotton off his shoulders.

'Perfect,' she said, running her fingers over his pecs. 'I've always thought you could be a model for any of the posh perfume houses.' She let her fingers slide down to his abdomen. 'And a perfect six pack.'

'Careful—my ego might explode.'

She laughed. 'You're not an egotist, Ellis.'

'Good.' He drew her closer and kissed her again, his

mouth warm and sweet and very sure. Then he broke the kiss and held her gaze. 'Right now, I want to kiss you all over.'

'Sounds good to me.' Her knees felt like jelly; she hadn't felt this nervous or this turned on in a long while.

'I'm glad. And, just so you know, I intend to take my time.'

The huskiness in his voice made the heat running through her gear up another notch.

He kissed from the corner of her mouth down to the curve of her jaw. Instinctively, she tipped her head back and he kissed his way down the side of her neck, teasing and inciting. She was aware of the pulse beating madly in her throat, and then his mouth skimmed it, skimmed it again, and nibbled and teased until she thought she was going to burst into flames with desire.

Then he straightened up again and traced the lacy edge of her bra with his fingertip, taking his own sweet time. Just as he'd promised.

'Do you have any idea how much I want you?' she whispered.

'I hope it's as much as I want you,' he said.

She smiled, and let him slide the straps of her bra down her arms. At work he was a total professional; nothing ever fazed him and his hands were steady and sure. Yet right now his hands were shaking and his breathing was shallow. Clearly he was as affected as much as she was by this thing between them.

He undid her bra strap and let the garment drift to the floor. 'You're so beautiful,' he said. 'And I want you so much I can't think straight.'

'Me, too,' she said, and lifted a hand to stroke his face.

He pressed a kiss into her palm, drew his hands down

her sides and then stroked upwards again so he could cup her breasts. His thumbs grazed her nipples and made her shiver.

She slid her hands into his hair; it felt soft and silky beneath her fingertips. Then she kissed him, pressing against him.

He pulled her closer and kissed her back.

Ruby wasn't sure who removed the rest of whose clothing, but the next thing she knew Ellis was carrying her to the wide, wide bed and had pushed the coverlet aside. He laid her down on the sheets; then she felt the mattress dip with his weight as he joined her.

'Ruby, you're so beautiful—everything I dreamed of and more.'

His fingers were feather-light as he touched her, making her skin feel hotter. He followed his hands with his mouth, and she arched against the bed.

'Now, Ellis,' she said. 'Please, now.'

She felt the bed dip again as he stood up and opened her eyes in shock. Had he changed his mind?

Then she realised that he was taking his wallet from his jacket, removing a foil package.

'Protection,' he said. 'And, just so you know, I wasn't making assumptions. Just being prepared.'

'Practical and sensible.'

'Which isn't,' he said as he joined her back on the bed, 'the same as boring.'

No, she didn't think this was going to be boring in the slightest.

She reached for him and kissed him hard.

This time, it felt safe to let the desire ignite. Her head fell back as he kissed his way down her body, exploring the hollows of her collar-bones and the valley between her breasts, stroking the soft undersides and making her sigh with pleasure.

She slid her fingers into his hair as he teased her nipples with the tip of his tongue. Then he drew the hard peak into his mouth and sucked.

'More,' she whispered, and he kissed his way downwards over her abdomen. She shivered. She wanted this so much; she couldn't remember the last time she'd wanted someone so desperately.

He shifted to kneel between her thighs. She felt him lift her foot and kiss the hollow of her ankle. As he worked his way slowly north, she felt as if her bones were dissolving; she was so ready for him.

She felt the slow stroke of one finger along her sex, and it made her whimper with need. And then he bent to replace his finger with his mouth. As his tongue flicked across her clitoris she completely lost it; her climax hit her like a wall.

Ruby was still almost hyperventilating as she finally opened her eyes.

Ellis held her close. 'Well. That was interesting.'

'Ellis...' Her brain felt scrambled and she couldn't even string two words together.

He just smiled. 'It's good to know that I can turn the smartest woman I know into mush.' His smile grew tinged with wickedness. 'But I haven't finished yet.'

'Better be a promise,' she mumbled.

'Oh, it is.' He kissed her again, touched her and stroked her until she was back at fever point, and then she heard the tear of the foil packet and the snap of the condom as he moved to protect her.

And then, finally, he eased inside her.

Incredibly, she felt her climax rising again.

And this time, when the wall hit her and she cried out, she heard his answering cry and felt his body surge against hers.

Afterwards, he said softly, 'I need to deal with the condom.'

'Sure.'

When he came back from the bathroom, he climbed back into bed beside her and drew her into his arms.

'Ellis, I...'

He pressed a finger lightly against her lips. 'Don't speak. Tonight, let's just be.'

And it had been so long since she'd slept in someone's arms. So long since she'd felt warm and safe and cherished.

She reached over to switch out the light, and cuddled into him. And finally she fell asleep in his arms.

Ellis lay awake for a while longer, just holding Ruby.

What had just happened between them had been a total revelation—a connection he'd never experienced with anyone else, even Natalia.

It gave him hope for the future. Maybe, just maybe, this thing between them would work out.

But, at the same time, it brought back all the panic. He'd thought that he loved Natalia, and that she'd felt the same about him. They'd been good together. Yet his marriage hadn't lasted—they'd discovered within weeks that they'd made a huge mistake because they wanted totally different things out of life.

What did Ruby want out of life? Another marriage like the one she'd had with Tom, perhaps, settled and close to both their families? He didn't know if he could offer her that. Would he be enough for her? Would he be able to suppress his wanderlust for her? Had he just made another huge mistake with the potential to hurt someone he cared about?

He smiled wryly. So much for telling her, 'Tonight, let's just be.' Instead of enjoying this moment, relaxing in the warmth and sweetness, he was full of doubts.

Maybe he should take his own advice, just for tonight, and live in the moment. Just be. Tomorrow there would be time for reflection. Tonight, he'd just enjoy holding her asleep in his arms.

CHAPTER ELEVEN

THE NEXT MORNING Ruby woke, feeling warm and comfortable. A surge of embarrassment heated her skin as she remembered last night, and then a flood of guilt washed away the embarrassment.

She felt a kiss against her shoulder. 'Ruby. Chill out,' Ellis said softly.

'How long have you been awake?' she asked, turning to face him.

'Long enough.' He stroked her face. 'What's the matter?'

She took a deep breath. 'You and me. Last night.'

'Problem?' His voice was neutral and his face was expressionless, so she didn't have a clue how he was feeling. Did he regret this? Did he think they should go back to being friends? Did he feel as mixed-up about this whole situation as she did?

'Yes. No.' She closed her eyes. 'I don't regret what we did. But I do feel guilty about it.'

'Why?' he asked gently. 'Ruby, we're both single. We have feelings for each other, and we simply acted on those feelings last night.'

'You're the first since Tom,' she whispered. 'The only one apart from Tom.'

'Which makes me feel incredibly honoured,' he said softly.

She opened her eyes then and looked at him. 'Honoured?'

'Honoured,' he repeated, 'that you chose me. Ruby, there's no need to feel guilty. You're not betraying Tom.'

'It feels like it,' she said.

He shook his head. 'Tom loved you enough to want you to be happy after he died. And you're not trying to push his memory out of your life. It's OK to move on. We've been dating for a few weeks and we've known each other for an awful lot longer than that.'

'I guess I'm being ridiculous.'

'No. You're human. You can't turn your feelings on and off just like that—neither of us can.'

'Are you saying that you feel guilty, too?'

'Technically, you're my best friend's girl,' he said. 'So, yes, in a way I do feel guilty. But I would never, ever have done anything to jeopardise your marriage if Tom had still been alive. Tom's been gone for more than a year now. I know we both still miss him and we always will, but we have to face up to the fact that he's gone. And I think he'd be pleased if we could find happiness together.' He gave her a rueful smile. 'Though I have to admit, he'd probably give me a huge lecture about commitment and making sure I don't hurt you.'

'Right now we can't promise each other for ever,' Ruby said.

'Which is fine,' Ellis reassured her. 'We can promise each other for now. Enjoy the moment.'

'While it lasts?'

'Which might be for longer than both of us think. If we're lucky.'

'I need to stop brooding,' she said wryly.

'And I need coffee,' he said. 'How long will it take you to shower?'

The glint in his eyes prompted her to say, 'That depends on whether I'm showering alone.'

He grinned. 'I like your thinking, Rubes. In fact...'

They were almost too late for breakfast. And Ellis didn't look quite as pristine as he normally did when he emerged from his room with his luggage, ready to go in the hotel's store-room until their taxi arrived to take them back to the airport.

'So, our last day in Prague,' he said when they'd checked out and had the receipts for their luggage. 'Where would you like to go?'

'You're the one with the guide book. Where do you suggest?'

'I'd like to take a closer look at the Dancing House,' he said. 'And there's this café where Einstein used to hang out.'

She laughed. 'And you want to follow in his footsteps?'

'Just for coffee. I think I'll pass on developing theories of relativity.' He laughed back.

They went to see the Dancing House, and Ellis persuaded another tourist to take a photograph on his phone of himself and Ruby in front of the building in the same dance pose. They walked along the river bank, hand in hand, enjoying the autumn sunshine, then found the café on Ellis's wish list. It was all chandeliers and gorgeous Viennese-style cake and coffee; and there were chess sets out on various tables with a note telling patrons to enjoy a game if they wished.

'Fancy a game?' Ellis asked.

Ruby shook her head. 'Sorry, I've never played.'

'I could teach you.'

'Thanks, but I don't think chess is for me.' She raised an eyebrow. 'Something else I didn't know about you, Ellis.'

'Me? I'm an open book,' he said lightly.

The bright morning sunshine had given way to threatening clouds by the time they'd finished their cake and coffee, so they spent the rest of the day in art galleries and museums, before collecting their luggage and meeting their taxi to the airport.

Prague would always have a special place in her heart, Ruby thought. The place where she and Ellis had first made love.

But, once they were back in England—what then? Would they stay close like this? Or would the world get in the way?

And there were other considerations, too. They weren't the only ones to think about.

She pushed it to the back of her head and chatted easily with Ellis all the way back to England.

Though he'd clearly been thinking about it too; when he saw her to her front door, he asked softly, 'So where do we go from here?'

'I don't know,' she said. 'What do you want?'

'Are you ready to go public?'

She wrinkled her nose. 'Don't take this the wrong way, but can I talk to Tom's parents about it first?'

'I think that would be kind,' he said, 'and I agree with you. If they're not comfortable with the situation, then we need to keep it to ourselves a little longer, until they've had time to get used to the idea.'

'Thank you. For understanding,' she said.

'Any time.' He kissed her lightly. 'I guess I'll see you at work tomorrow.'

'Yes. And thank you for Prague. It was special.'

'It was,' he agreed. And for a moment she could swear that she saw sadness in his eyes.

'You're twenty-two weeks, according to your scan, Mrs Falcon,' Ellis said gently.

'I really can't get my head round this.' Anita Falcon shook her head. 'I'm forty-five years old. I'm a professional. I've got a fifteen-year-old. How could I possibly not realise I was pregnant again, until last week?' She shook her head. 'I've seen the newspaper stories about women who don't have a clue they're pregnant until they actually have the baby. I always thought that was crazy—I mean, if you're pregnant you get morning sickness, your periods stop, you have a definite bump and you can feel the baby moving. How can you not *know*? I just…' She shook her head, and a tear trickled down her face. 'Ten years ago, I would've been thrilled. It'd be a dream come true, being able to give Max a little brother or sister. But how can I possibly cope with a baby now, when I have my parents living with me, and my dad has dementia, and my son is going to be doing his exams next June? Not to mention Nick—my husband—might be made redundant next month, so we can't afford for me to give up my job, even if it's only for a few months. And it's so late now that even if I could face the idea of a termination, it's not going to be possible. It's my own stupid fault for not having a clue.' She covered her face with her hands, and Ruby could see her shoulders heaving with sobs.

She sat down next to Anita and put her arm round

her. 'Hey. Don't beat yourself up. There are plenty of reasons why a woman might not realise she's pregnant. From what you've just told me, you're under quite a bit of stress right now.'

Anita rubbed the tears away from her eyes with the back of her hand. 'It's been hard to get the right help for Dad. Dealing with the authorities is like banging your head against a brick wall. We all want him to keep his independence as much as possible, and I wanted to take the strain off Mum—that's why they moved in with us.'

'It's difficult, sharing a home with your parents again after years of not living with them,' Ellis said. 'And it's doubly hard if they're not in the best of health. You're worrying about them, and you're worrying about your son as well—and your husband's job.'

'I thought it was just stress mucking my system up,' Anita said. 'I haven't had a period for four months—but my periods were a bit all over the place before that, so I just assumed I was heading for the menopause. The same as having to get up at night for a wee; I thought it was my age. I went and had a chat with the local pharmacist, and she said she was the same age as me and it was probably nothing to worry about, but do a pregnancy test just to put my mind at rest.'

'Good idea,' Ellis said.

She dragged in a breath. 'Back when I was pregnant with Max, you just had a blue line on the test stick and you had to guess whether it was a dark enough blue to be a positive result. Nowadays, the tests have a screen that tells you how pregnant you are—and the one I did definitely said "not pregnant". So I thought it was OK, that I was right about my system being all over the place with menopause and stress.'

'Sometimes you can get a false negative result on a test,' Ruby said. 'Though you're right. A lot of women hit the perimenopause at your age and your periods go all over the place.'

'I haven't had any morning sickness,' Anita said, 'and I was terrible when I had Max. Even tin cans used to smell and make me feel queasy. Right from the second week to the twelfth, when I was pregnant with him, I had to run to the bathroom if someone came into work wearing really strong aftershave or hairspray. This time, there was nothing. Not the slightest bit.'

'Your body doesn't always react the same way in pregnancy. Some women have horrendous morning sickness with one baby and nothing at all with another. How about your weight?' Ellis asked. 'Has that changed much?'

'I've put on about ten pounds.' Anita grimaced. 'Though I put that down to middle-age spread. And stress. I haven't exactly been eating brilliantly—when the going gets tough, the tough get chocolate, right?'

'Right,' Ruby said. 'Some women don't put on that much weight during pregnancy. If they're doing a lot of exercise—say they're training for a marathon—or they're overweight to start with, the pregnancy might not show for quite a while.'

'Plus, if you have a uterus that tips back the other way—as one in five women do—you wouldn't have noticed a bump anyway for at least the first twelve weeks,' Ellis said.

Anita stared at them, the tiniest bit of hope on her face. 'So I wasn't just being stupid, not realising I was pregnant?'

'You weren't being stupid at all,' Ruby reassured

her. 'And there's a fifteen-year gap between your pregnancies, so your body won't remember what it feels
like to have a baby moving around inside. Plus you've
been worried sick about quite a lot of things, and you
haven't been looking out for the signs of being pregnant. So that'd be why you missed that little fluttering
of the baby moving.'

'I did have terrible heartburn last week. I never had
that when I was pregnant with Max. I thought it was
just a combination of stress and comfort eating, and I
knew I ought to be doing something about my weight
but I just couldn't face it, not with everything else going
on. Chocolate is the only thing that's kept me sane. I
couldn't believe it when my GP said he thought I might
be pregnant.' Anita bit her lip. 'And I've been eating
all the wrong things—soft cheese, lightly cooked eggs,
wine. I haven't taken any folic acid, I've been eating
rubbish instead of really nutritious food, and...' She
broke off, clearly fighting back the tears.

'And you're panicking that you've harmed the baby,'
Ellis said. 'But what I saw on the scan was a baby who's
the right size for dates, has ten fingers and toes, and
has a steadily beating heart. I didn't see anything that
would worry me, as an obstetrician. Plus you still have
another eighteen weeks or so to eat green leafy vegetables until they're coming out of your ears.'

'You bet I will.' Anita gave him a wobbly smile. 'So
I'm not the only woman who's ever done that?'

'Far from it,' Ellis said with a smile. 'And it will take
a bit of getting used to. Do you have other family who
can support you?'

'An older brother,' Anita said. 'But he sticks his head
in the sand about Mum and Dad, so he won't do any-

thing to help me with them. He's always got an excuse not to visit us. And it's not even as if he lives over the other side of the country.'

Guilt prickled the back of Ellis's neck. Over the years he'd had plenty of excuses not to visit his parents. Mainly because he worked so far away.

'Families aren't always easy,' he said feelingly. 'How about your husband's family?'

'Let's just say how much my mother-in-law will enjoy telling people that I'm supposed to be so clever, but I was too stupid to know I was pregnant and too stupid to know how to use contraception,' Anita said wryly. 'But I do have the best friend in the universe. She'll be there for me. And I think, once Max and Nick get over the shock, they'll be there for me, too.'

Ruby squeezed her hand. 'That's great. And you've also got us. Anything you're worried about between your appointments, come and talk to us. We have a walk-in clinic here in the department as well as the regular appointments.'

'Thank you.' Anita took a deep breath. 'I'm sorry I've been so wet. Crying and all that. That just isn't me.'

'Hormones,' Ruby said sagely. 'Plus you have a lot on your plate. In your shoes, I'd be just the same.'

'Really?'

'Really.' Ruby patted her shoulder. 'Right. Let's finish doing your checks, and we'll make another appointment for you in two weeks' time—we want to keep a closer eye on you simply because you're an older mum, not because there's anything to panic about. But if you're worried about anything in the meantime, come and see us.'

'You've been so kind about this. Both of you. I mean,

you have to see this stupid, ditzy woman who doesn't even know she's pregnant until she's over halfway through...'

'Don't put yourself down,' Ellis said. 'Actually,' he added, 'studies show that about one in about five hundred women don't realise they're pregnant until they're twenty weeks gone, so you're not stupid at all.'

'Thank you. Both of you.' She took a deep breath. 'This baby wasn't planned, but it's never going to feel unwanted.'

Later that evening, Ellis and Ruby were curled up together on his sofa.

'That poor woman who came to see us this afternoon,' she said. 'She's got a huge amount to deal with.'

'A late baby's tough for anyone, but she's caring for her parents as well, and she's supporting her son through his GCSEs and worrying about her husband's job. It's hardly surprising she was too stressed to notice the signs of pregnancy,' Ellis said.

'If I was in her situation,' Ruby said, 'I'd have to leave London and go back to Manchester. I couldn't leave my parents to struggle, and I wouldn't want to uproot them from everything that's familiar and make them move to London with me. I'm an only child, so there's nobody else to pick up the slack or share it with me.'

'If it happened to my parents, they'd be difficult about it,' Ellis said. 'I think they'd hide how much they were struggling and they'd stonewall the three of us if we asked any questions.' He sighed. 'I worry about them. So do my brothers. But we can't force them to be close to us or accept more help than they're prepared to take.'

'And I guess when you're working hundreds and hundreds of miles away, rushed off your feet and with a million different things to think about, it helps fill in the gaps so you don't have as much space to worry,' she said softly.

'You mean, I use my job to escape? There's a lot of truth in that,' he said ruefully. 'And I feel a bit ashamed of myself for that. I thought about that when Anita was telling us how her brother makes excuses not to visit. I guess I do, too.'

'Ellis, you're human,' she said, stroking his face. 'We all have our limitations. And you can't save everyone or fix things for everyone.'

'I know.' He kissed her lightly. 'Some things can't be fixed. And you have to put up with the fact that you're doing everything you can, even if it doesn't feel anywhere near enough.'

'I wish I had a magic wand,' she said.

'Me, too. But thank you for making me feel better about it.'

'I haven't done anything.'

'You have. I can talk to you and know you're not judging me. That makes a huge difference.'

'Oh, Ellis.' Her eyes sparkled with tears.

'Hey. Let's change the subject now and talk about something nice.'

'Brenda and Mike are coming up to London, next weekend.' Ruby paused. 'I think it's time to tell them about us.'

'With me by your side,' he said. 'I love Tom's parents. Even if you and I weren't together, I would've probably asked if I could drop in just to say hello to them.' He stroked her face. 'But now you and I are together, of course I want to be there and help you tell them.' He stole a kiss. 'And I'm also hoping that I can persuade you to stay here with me tonight.'

'I don't have anything with me.'

'I have a spare toothbrush, practically all the toiletries you'll need except face cream—and taking one night off isn't going to give you immediate wrinkles—and I can always put your clothes through the washing machine now so they'll be clean and dry in the morning. Your uniform's kept at work, you don't have a dog or cat to go back and feed, and I do a seriously mean scrambled egg on toast. Oh, and freshly squeezed orange juice—and I mean freshly squeezed by me, not poured from a bottle.'

She laughed. 'Very persuasive, Dr Webster. I have no arguments against any of that. I'd love to stay.'

'Good.' He kissed her again. Another step towards the relationship he thought they were both looking for. Another reason to stay in London. At the same time, though, it scared him. He knew Ruby so much better than he'd known Natalie. They were compatible in every way. And yet the doubts were still there. He'd failed at his last marriage—his last serious relationship. Would he fail at this one, too?

CHAPTER TWELVE

'I FEEL RIDICULOUSLY NERVOUS,' Ruby said on the Sunday morning.

'It'll be fine. Don't worry,' Ellis reassured her.

'I guess.' But she couldn't help feeling antsy. She wanted to be with Ellis—but she also didn't want to lose Brenda and Mike. Once they knew she was dating again, would they reject her?

The doorbell rang; Ruby opened the door and Brenda and Mike greeted her with a hug and flowers.

'Oh, Ellis, you're here too—how lovely to see you as well.' Brenda hugged him and Mike shook his hand warmly.

'Can I get you some coffee?' Ruby asked.

'That'd be wonderful,' Brenda said.

'I'll make the coffee,' Ellis offered.

'And I'll put these lovely flowers in water,' Ruby said with a smile.

'When are we going to tell them?' Ruby whispered in the kitchen.

'I vote for sooner rather than later,' Ellis whispered back.

'OK. I'll be brave,' she said.

Once they were all sitting down in the living room

with coffee and posh cookies that Ruby had bought from the deli round the corner, she said, 'There was something I wanted to talk to you about.'

'Of course, love,' Mike said.

Ruby took a deep breath. 'Please don't think I'll ever forget Tom or push him out of my life, but—'

'—you've met someone,' Brenda cut in gently.

Ruby stared at her, surprised. Was it that obvious? 'Um, yes,' she said awkwardly.

'Love, it's been more than a year since he died and you're still young. I'm quite sure Tom didn't want you to spend the rest of your life on your own, missing him,' Brenda said.

'So you don't mind if I see someone?' Ruby asked.

'As long as he treats you right,' Mike said. 'If he isn't good to you, then I'll have a problem with it.'

'That won't be a problem,' Ellis said. 'Remember, Tom asked me to take care of her.'

'Have you met Ruby's young man, then?' Brenda asked.

Ellis coughed. 'Let's just say you've known him for quite a few years, too.'

They both stared at him, and he saw the second that the penny dropped. The surprise in their faces was swiftly chased away by relief.

'But,' he said, 'we didn't want to go public until we knew you were OK with it.'

'We're OK with it,' Brenda said softly. 'More than OK.'

Mike smiled. 'I wish we'd brought champagne now.'

'Actually, I did, hoping that I wasn't tempting fate,' Ellis said. 'Though if you hadn't been OK with Ruby seeing me, then I would've suggested using it to toast our Tom. Shall I go and open it?'

'Absolutely yes,' Brenda said. 'And we wish you both every happiness, we really do.'

Later that evening, Ellis and Ruby lay together on her sofa.

'I'm so glad they were OK about us,' she said.

'Me, too. So are you ready to go public tomorrow?' he asked.

'I think so.' She looked awkward. 'I probably ought to confess that I told Tina, a while back.'

Her best friend. Would she approve? 'And was she OK about it?' Ellis asked, careful to keep his voice neutral.

'Actually, she brought up your itchy feet.' She sighed. 'And she told me not to fall for you too hard or too fast.'

'My feet aren't itchy,' Ellis said, 'but it looks as if I'm going to need to convince you of that—and a few other people, too.'

She stroked his face. 'It's not that I doubt you. But you're used to moving about all the time.'

'I've stayed in London for well over a year and a half now,' he pointed out.

'Don't you miss it, working abroad and seeing different places all the time?' she asked.

'Yes. But I'm pretty sure I'd miss you more,' he said softly.

The news gradually spread round the hospital. Ruby was surprised and pleased that everyone seemed to wish them both well, especially when they made it clear that the personal relationship would make absolutely no difference to their professional relationship.

The next morning, Ellis came over to the midwives' station to show Ruby a letter from Grace Edwards. 'You know you thought she might be a chimera? She had more DNA tests, and they showed that you were right. The court case has been settled now, and she says the relationship with her ex is starting to become more amicable for the child's sake.'

'That's good. I'm so glad it's working out better for her now.'

Ellis stole a kiss. 'Not just for her. Everything's working out. I never would've believed I could be so happy.'

'Me, too.' She kissed him back.

'Tsk, you two, you're supposed to set a good example to your juniors,' Coral, the trainee midwife, teased as she passed them.

Ellis just laughed. 'We are.'

Over the next few weeks, time seemed to go at the speed of light. Ellis and Ruby spent every possible minute together. But finally it was his last official day at the maternity unit. That evening, all the staff from the unit who weren't on duty went out for a pizza to say goodbye to him, and presented him with a special care package for his trip to Zimbabwe—including socks, chocolate and soap, which made him laugh—and a card signed by every single person on the team.

'We want you back, Ellis,' Theo said. 'No pressure, of course, but we want you back. And I'm expecting the answer to a certain question the second you get back on English soil.'

In other words, whether he'd accept the job offer. Ellis smiled. 'OK. Message received and understood.'

'And we want regular texts to know how you're getting on,' Iris, the senior midwife, chipped in.

'Actually, I'm not going to be able to be in touch with anyone while I'm away,' Ellis said. 'This clinic I'm going to in Zimbabwe is so remote that there isn't any Internet access, and there's no mobile phone coverage.'

Ruby swallowed hard. He'd already told her this, so she was prepared for it, but it was still hard to get her head round it.

'So I guess sending us the odd postcard won't be possible either?' She tried for levity.

'By the time I'd found someone to take a letter to the nearest big town with a mail system and buy a stamp for it—well, I'd probably be back here before the postcard reached you, even if I sent it on my first day.'

It finally hit home. No phone, no texts, no emails, and not even a letter. A whole month without contact. She trusted Ellis—she knew he wasn't the kind to cheat—but how did people cope with the loneliness of long-distance relationships like this, when they couldn't even contact each other for weeks at a time? Was this the way her future was going to be?

She changed the subject and teased Ellis along with the rest of the team, but when they went back to his flat afterwards he held her close.

'Rubes, I know it's going to be hard, not being able to talk to each other for a whole month,' he said. 'But if there's an emergency, you know you can call John at the medical aid charity and he'll get someone to radio a message through to me,' said. 'And, if you really want me to, I can pull out of the assignment.'

He'd really do that for her?

She could see the sincerity in his eyes. Yes, he'd give it up for her.

But she couldn't ask him to do that. Especially on the day before he was meant to be going. She shook her head. 'You promised you'd go. I'm not going to make you break a promise.' She just wished there could be another way.

Though the only other way she could think of was for her to go with him. Which would mean letting down everyone at the ward, and deserting her family, Brenda and Mike. She couldn't do that, either.

And giving Ellis an ultimatum wasn't fair; it would tear him apart. She knew he was a man of integrity. He was going back to do the job he loved—maybe for the last assignment. Or maybe not. For his sake she needed to be brave about this. To make him feel that it was okay for him to go—even though watching him leave would hurt like hell. 'Go get 'em, tiger.' She gave him a wobbly smile.

That night, they made love for what might be the last time, and the sweetness was almost unbearable. Ruby just hoped that Ellis wasn't aware of the tears trickling silently down her face as she lay awake in his arms afterwards, pretending to sleep.

The next day, Ruby went to see Ellis off at the airport.

She looked at the kitbag slung over his shoulder as they left his flat. 'I can't believe that's all the luggage you're taking with you for a whole month.'

'I learned to travel light.' He smiled at her. 'Ruby, I *am* coming back, you know.'

'I know.' His assignment was for a month. Of course

he was coming back. But would it be for good, or would it be to tell her that he'd rediscovered how much he loved his job and he needed to go back to it?

'Ruby, I lo—'

She pressed the tip of her finger against his mouth. She had a feeling she knew what he was going to say— and she didn't want to hear it. Not right at this moment. 'Wait until you're back,' she said softly. Until he'd been away from her and had had time to think about it. Until he really knew what he wanted to do—whether he needed to go back to working abroad, or whether he wanted to come back to London to stay. If he could still say it in a month's time, then she'd know that he really meant it.

They travelled to Heathrow on the train in silence, and had a last cup of coffee together while they waited for his flight to be called.

And then the flight to Harare was announced over the tannoy system.

'I guess this is me,' he said. He held her tightly. 'I'll see you in a month. And I'll be counting the days. I'll think of you every single day.'

'Me, too.' She wasn't going to cry. She wasn't going to let him go on that plane feeling guilty and miserable because of her. 'You go and you make that difference to the world. I'm proud of you.' And she was proud of him. Just… she didn't want him to go. 'I'll keep an eye on your flat for you and make sure you've got fresh bread and milk indoors when you get back.' She dragged in a breath. 'And I'll see you in a month's time.'

'I'll ring you as soon as I can switch my phone on and get a signal.' His grey eyes were tortured. 'Ruby. I wish I wasn't going.'

'If you don't go, you'll regret it for the rest of your life. So go. Do what you're brilliant at. Help set up that clinic and make life better for people.' Go with her love, though she wasn't going to say that and put pressure on him. 'Have a safe journey,' she said. Though she wouldn't even know if he did arrive safely. She could check the airport website to see if he'd landed; and then she'd just have to trust that everything went well after that. That any unrest in the country wouldn't affect the clinic. That he wouldn't catch some awful virus. *That he'd come back.*

A whole month without him.

And it stretched out as if there was never going to be an end.

'Ruby.' His voice sounded as clogged as her throat felt.

He kissed her hard. 'I'll be back soon,' he said.

'I know.' Even though she didn't know whether it would be just to say goodbye, or to tell her that he wanted to be with her.

She waited in the airport until his flight had taken off, even though she knew he wouldn't be able to make her out through the window. She just needed to be there until he'd finally gone.

And just why was the sun shining so brightly on the train home? Why wasn't it miserable and raining, the way it felt in her heart?

The following day, Ruby went to see one of their new mums, whose baby had been born at thirty-six weeks and now, at three days old, the baby had a distinct yellow tone to her eyes and skin. For a moment, Ruby wished Ellis was there, because he was so good at explaining things like this to new parents. Then she pulled herself together. Ellis wasn't there; this was her job, and she was just going to have to deal with it.

'Basically the baby has a bit too much bilirubin in her body—that's why her skin and her eyes have that yellow tinge,' she explained.

'What's bilirubin?' Mrs Patterson asked.

'It's a yellow substance the body makes when red blood cells—the ones that move oxygen round the body—break down. Usually the liver removes the bilirubin from the blood—actually, your liver did the job for her while she was still in the womb. Three out of five babies have a bit of jaundice—that's why we do that heel-prick test on the first day, to check her blood. She's quite jaundiced, and Coral tells me that you've had a bit of a problem feeding her.'

'So is it my fault?'

'Not at all,' Ruby reassured her. 'The jaundice explains why she's not feeding well.'

'So will she have to have medication to treat it?'

'Believe it or not, the treatment's a bit of sunshine— but at this time of year there isn't much sunshine around, so what we're going to do is fibre-optic phototherapy,' Ruby said. 'Which is a fancy way of saying we're going to lie her on a blanket which shines a special light onto her back. Her skin will absorb the light and it makes oxygen bind to the bilirubin, helping it dissolve so her liver can break it down.'

Mrs Patterson looked surprised. 'That's all? You just lay her on a special blanket?'

'And we keep checking the levels of bilirubin in her blood until they start dropping. It does mean she's going to lose a bit more water from her body than usual, so we might have to give her some fluid in a drip to keep her hydrated—but basically that's it, and you can be with her the whole time. You can still feed her as normal and change her nappies,' Ruby explained. 'She'll be much better in a day or two.'

'And then she's going to be all right?'

'She's going to be just fine,' Ruby confirmed.

It was true for the baby; and if she kept telling herself often enough that everything was going to be fine, then it would be true for her and Ellis, too.

Ellis was really glad that the pace in Zimbabwe turned out to be punishing. Being so busy that he didn't have time to think about how much he missed Ruby was a blessing—as was being so tired that he fell asleep almost as soon as his head touched the pillow at night. And although he was friendly with the other medics on the team, he didn't socialise as much as he would have done in the old days. Instead, he spent every evening writing to Ruby, in a notebook he'd bought especially for the purpose. He wouldn't be able to send her a postcard or a letter every day, but he would at least be able to give her the book when he returned. So she'd know that he'd meant what he'd said—that he'd thought about her every single day when he was away.

On his last day, he had a radio call from John, the assignment handler at the medical aid charity. 'Ellis, I know it's a lot to ask, but could you stay a bit longer? A couple of weeks?'

Two years ago, he would've said yes without even having to think about it. Extending an assignment was something he'd done quite a few times.

Now, it was different. He'd spent a whole month

missing Ruby and it was like a physical ache. He loved what he did, but the job wasn't enough for him any more. Not without Ruby.

Because he loved her.

Bone-deep *loved* her.

And he needed to be back with her.

'I'm sorry,' Ellis said. 'But no. Don't get me wrong—I love this job, but I've met someone. In London. And now I need to go home. For good.' He was shocked to feel the lump in his throat: London *was* home. Because Ruby was there.

As long as she hadn't changed her mind about them while he'd been away.

'Fair enough,' John said. 'It sounds as if we've been lucky to have you back for the last month.'

'I promised I'd do this assignment,' Ellis said, 'and I wouldn't break my promise.' Even though he'd been tempted to. He'd done the right thing.

'We'll miss you,' John said. 'And if you ever change your mind—even if it's just for a few days—we'd have you back any time.'

'You'll be the first to know,' Ellis said.

CHAPTER THIRTEEN

ELLIS HAD DELIBERATELY given Ruby the wrong date for his return; he'd told her that he'd be back the day after his real return date, knowing from experience how likely it was that his journey home would be disrupted. In the past he'd worried his brothers by turning up later than they expected, and he didn't want Ruby to be anxious about whether something had happened to him when he wasn't in a position to get in touch with her.

The journey home seemed to take for ever—from the journey by jeep from the camp through to the airport in Harare, and then the flight itself. With two layovers, it took the best part of a whole day to fly back to England. And every minute felt like a lifetime.

As soon as Ellis was through passport control at Heathrow, he got his phone out of his pocket. But somehow he managed to fumble it, and it dropped to the floor. When he picked it up, he groaned. 'You've got to be *kidding* me! How am I going to ring Ruby now?'

'Got a problem, mate?' a voice said beside him.

Ellis turned to face his fellow passenger and ruefully showed him the cracked screen. 'I've managed to baby this thing for a whole month while I've been setting up a clinic in an incredibly remote area, but as soon as I'm back here I drop it just once and...' He shook his head. 'What an idiot.'

'Here, use mine.' The man handed Ellis his phone.

'Are you sure?' At the other man's nod, Ellis smiled. 'Thank you very much. I'll keep it quick and I'll pay you for the call.'

'It's fine, mate. I know how I'd feel if I'd been away and couldn't ring my missus to tell her I'd landed safely.'

'Yeah. I told her I'd be back tomorrow because I didn't want her worrying if I was held up. And I just can't wait any longer to talk to her.' He opened the screen to dial Ruby's number, and stopped. 'Oh, no. I don't believe this. I can't actually remember her mobile number. How stupid am I?'

The other man gave him a rueful smile. 'That's where these things fall down, isn't it? We rely on them to remember everything for us, and when they don't work we're stuck.'

'Very true,' Ellis said, equally ruefully. Plus, after more than twenty-four hours spent travelling, he could barely think straight. All he wanted was to go home and see Ruby.

He handed the phone back to the other man. 'Thank you anyway. I appreciate the offer.'

'I hope you manage to get hold of her.'

'I'll find a way,' Ellis said.

Once he'd walked through customs to the airport shopping complex, he found the nearest shop that sold mobile phones. 'How long does it take to fix one of these?' he asked, showing the assistant his cracked screen.

'At least until tomorrow, I'm afraid,' the assistant told him.

Not what he needed to hear. Time for Plan B. 'Okay, how long would it take to migrate all my data across to a new phone?'

'The guy who does that sort of thing won't be in for another couple of hours, and he might already have stuff to do, so I can't say.'

A couple of hours and then unlimited waiting? No chance. Ellis knew he could be back in the centre of London, actually *with* Ruby, in the time it'd take to sort out his phone so he could call her. 'Thanks, but I'll manage. Can I just buy a cheap pay-as-you-go phone to tide me over until I can get this one fixed?'

'Sure.'

Armed with a working phone, Ellis managed to get the hospital switchboard number from the Internet, and two seconds later he was patched through to the maternity ward.

'Hey, Iris. Don't say a word—it's Ellis. Is Ruby there?'

'Yes, she is. I thought you weren't due back until tomorrow?'

'My journey home was a bit smoother than I expected,' Ellis explained. 'What shift is she on?'

'Early.'

'Excellent. Can you keep her there, please? And don't tell her that you've spoken to me. I want to surprise her.'

He knew he was taking a risk. He'd missed Ruby like hell. Hopefully she'd missed him just as much—but on the other hand she might have had time to think about the situation and decided that she couldn't cope with his lifestyle. He knew she didn't want to join him in working abroad; and he knew she was scared that he'd feel trapped if she asked him to stay in London. But, while he'd been away, he'd come to his own decision. One that he hoped would work for her, too.

'I'll do my best,' Iris said.

'Thank you. I'll be there as soon as I can.'

The good thing about travelling light meant that it wasn't too much of a drag to carry his kitbag around. He caught the fast train back to central London, and then the tube across the city to the London Victoria. He paused only to buy the biggest bunch of flowers that the hospital shop could offer, then headed up to the maternity ward.

Iris was at the reception desk. 'Welcome home. Perfect timing—she's in the staff kitchen, and I'm pretty sure she's on her own,' she whispered with a wink.

'Thanks.' Ellis blew her a kiss and went straight to the staff kitchen.

Ruby was leaning against the counter, sipping a mug of coffee; she almost dropped it when she saw him. 'Ellis! I thought you weren't back until tomorrow!'

'Sometimes the flights get delayed—and I didn't want you having to hang around the airport for hours waiting for me, worrying that something terrible had happened. That's why I told you I'd be back tomorrow instead of today.' He placed the flowers on the counter, dropped his kitbag, swept her into his arms and swung her around. 'I've missed you so, so much,' he whispered and kissed her hard.

She matched him kiss for kiss, and her arms were wrapped as tightly round him as his were round her.

When he finally managed to break the kiss, he noticed that her skin was reddened. 'Oh God, I'm so sorry. The beard. I should have shaved first—and had a shower.' He grimaced. 'Sorry. I'm not exactly fragrant.'

She laughed. 'Don't worry. The main thing is that you're here. How long did it take you to get here?'

'Six hours in the jeep from the clinic to Harare, a bit of a wait there, nearly twenty hours from there to Heathrow in between layovers, and then way too long to get back to the middle of London.' He dragged in a breath. 'I was going to call you from Heathrow, but I dropped my phone. Would you believe, it was fine all through Zimbabwe, yet I managed to break it practically the second I was back in England?' He rolled his eyes. 'The guy next to me was really kind and lent me his phone—and then I couldn't remember your number. How stupid is that?'

She stroked his face. 'If it makes you feel any better, I don't think I can remember your mobile phone number, either—I rely on my phone to remember it for me.'

He moved his head so he could drop a kiss in her palm. 'I missed you so much. I know you stopped me saying it at the airport when you waved me off, and I know why, but I need to say it now. I love you, Ruby. I love you so much. And I want to stay here in London with you.'

'Ellis, you've been away for a month. You've been travelling for what, a day and a half, you probably haven't had much sleep, and this is a conversation I think we need to have when you're properly awake.'

Her voice was gentle, but fear trickled through him. Had he totally misread the situation? Had she changed her mind about their relationship while he'd been away?

She fished in the pockets of her trousers and brought out her door keys. 'Your flat is probably freezing cold, and you won't have any food in the fridge—I was going to sort all that out this evening, because I was expecting you back tomorrow and I thought I'd have time to do it tonight. I'll get my spare key from Tina. So why don't you just go back to my place, have a shower and get some sleep, and I'll see you when I get back after my shift? Help yourself to whatever you want from the fridge.'

'Thank you.' He put her keys carefully into his pocket. 'I wrote to you every day while I was away.' He opened his kitbag and took out the small notebook he'd carried everywhere with him. 'I thought it would be easier to write everything in here than carry around loads of bits of paper that I'd probably end up losing.' He handed her the notebook. 'It could be a bit of lunchtime reading for you.'

She went pink. 'You wrote to me every day?'

'Every single day,' he confirmed. 'It was the only way I had to be close to you when I was thousands of miles away.'

'I missed you so much.' Her voice sounded rusty. 'Ellis, I love you too.'

Everything in his world settled and felt right again. They felt the same way about each other—so somehow they would be able to work things out.

He wrapped his arms around her again and held her close. 'You're right, I need some sleep,' he said softly. 'But when I wake up, you'll be home with me. And then we can talk.' He kissed her lightly, then took the notebook back from her, went to the last page he'd written and carefully removed it.

'What are you doing?' she asked.

'When you read this particular page, I want to be with you,' he said. Then he remembered the flowers. He scooped them up from the counter and handed them to her. 'For you. I know they're not the best, but I just wanted to...' Right now, he was too tired to string words together.

'They're lovely, Ellis. You've been travelling for hours and hours and hours, and yet you still made the time to bring me flowers.' She kissed him again. 'Go home. Sleep. I'll see you soon.' She hugged him one last time. 'Welcome back. And I'm so, so pleased to see you.'

Her smile warmed him all the way back to her flat.

Ellis just about managed to shower and shave, though he couldn't quite face making himself anything to eat. He cleaned his teeth, then dragged himself into the spare bedroom—where he'd slept so many times before during Tom's final illness—and fell into oblivion almost the second that his head hit the pillow.

Ruby was glad that she hadn't arranged to have lunch with anyone. Right at that moment, she wanted to be on her own to read Ellis's letters to her. With the notebook stowed safely in her handbag, she went to the hospital canteen to buy a sandwich and some coffee, then found a table in a quiet corner and settled down to read.

The letters read almost like a diary. Ellis told her all about setting up the clinic, what the rest of the team was like, and told her about some of the patients he'd treated. Yet it wasn't just a practical day by day account of his life out there—he also wrote down his feelings. How much he missed her while he was away, how he'd always loved being able to make a difference to the world through his work and yet it just didn't feel right any more being away from London. How he'd looked up at the stars at night and thought of her, then realised they weren't even going to see the same stars because they weren't in the same hemisphere, and it made him feel lonely.

There was a huge lump in her throat. So his feelings for her hadn't changed. He really had missed her while he'd been away—and it looked as if there was a real chance that they had a future together.

Right at that moment, Ruby just wanted to be home with Ellis. Though she still had a whole afternoon until her shift was over. She was kept busy with clinics, but even so the time seemed to drag.

And then finally she was able to go off duty and go home. When she let herself into the flat, everything was silent. She walked quietly through to her bedroom, but Ellis wasn't sleeping in her bed. Clearly he was still being sensitive to her feelings and not sleeping where his best friend had once lain.

Even more quietly, Ruby opened the door to the spare room. Ellis was fast asleep, and she could see the tiredness and strain still etched on his face. Although part of her wanted to wake him up, she knew that it wouldn't be fair; he needed some rest to recover from all that travelling. She could see his kitbag on the floor, so there was at least one thing she could do for him; without waking him, she picked it up and quietly closed the door behind her.

The next thing Ellis knew, there were faint sounds coming from the flat. Clearly Ruby was at home, bustling about and yet trying her hardest not to wake him. Wishing he'd thought to call back at his flat first to get some clean clothes, he climbed out of bed, wearing only his boxer shorts, and bent down to where he'd left his kitbag.

Except there was an empty space where he was expecting to see it.

Had he left it in the bathroom, too tired to carry it in here? But it wasn't there, either.

Ruby must have heard him walking about because she called, 'Hey, Ellis?'

'Hey, yourself,' he said, following the sound of her voice and finding her in the kitchen. 'Sorry, I can't quite remember where I left my clothes.'

She smiled. 'In your kitbag, and at the moment they're most of the way through the washing cycle.'

'So basically I'm wearing the only clothes I have that are dry?' he asked.

'I thought you'd sleep a bit longer and they'd be ready by the time you woke up.' She looked guilty. 'Obviously I've been really noisy. Sorry I didn't mean to wake you.'

'You didn't wake me.' He wrapped her in his arms. 'Ruby, I'm so glad to be home.'

As the words left his mouth, he realised how much he meant it. London *was* home. He hadn't felt like that about a place for a very long time—since before Sally died, really—and it felt strange. Strange, but good.

'I'm glad to have you home,' she said. 'You must be starving.'

'I think I'm still too tired to be hungry,' he admitted. 'Right now, I just want to be with you. Though I could do with a cup of tea.' He glanced down at himself. 'And I'm really not respectable enough to be standing in your kitchen.'

'I gave all Tom's clothes to the charity shop,' she said, 'so I can't offer you anything of his to wear, and I don't think my dressing gown would fit you.'

He laughed. 'And I'm not sure pink's my colour anyway.'

'The best I can do is a towel, if you're cold.'

'I'm not cold. Just...' He paused. 'Maybe a little underdressed.'

'The view's quite nice from where I'm standing.' she said, and he loved the way colour stole into her face.

'The view's very nice from where I'm standing, too,' he said, and kissed her lingeringly.

Between them, they managed to make two mugs of tea, then sat down at her kitchen table.

'Did you read the notebook?' he asked.

She nodded. 'Every single page—except the one you took out.'

'Which I put in my...' A nasty thought hit him. 'Rubes, did you empty my pockets before you put my jeans in the washing machine?'

She went white. 'No.'

'Ah.'

'Are you saying I put your last letter to me through the wash?' She clapped a hand to her mouth. 'Oh, no. I can't have done.' Tears glistened in her eyes. 'Now I'll never know what you said.'

'I remember every word I wrote,' he said softly. 'I wanted to be there when you read them, but maybe it's better this way—with me telling you. I missed you out in Zimbabwe, Ruby. There was this big hole in my life, and my job just wasn't enough any more. On my very last day, John put a radio call through to the clinic, and he asked me if I'd stay on for a couple more weeks. Two years ago, I would've said yes without even hesitating. But this time I said no. Because I wanted to come home, Ruby. I wanted to come home to you. I wanted to be with you.'

He slid out of his chair and on to one knee in front of her. 'This isn't where I planned to do this. I was planning to find somewhere romantic—maybe somewhere by the sea, or maybe in one of the glasshouses at Kew with some exotic flowers in the background.' He gave her a wry smile. 'And I was going to be properly dressed. But as I was sitting on the plane, I knew exactly what I was going to say to you, and now I realise that it doesn't matter where I say it or what I'm wearing—and I don't want to wait any more. I love you, Ruby. I want to be with you. I don't want to go back to my old life, working abroad, because it just isn't enough for me any more. I've found the one person who makes me want to settle down—you. And I want to make a family with you, here in London. You're the love of my life. Will you marry me?'

She paused for so long that he thought she was going to say no.

And then, very shakily, she said, 'Yes.'

That was when Ellis realised that he'd actually been holding his breath.

He dragged in a lungful of air, then got to his feet, pulled her out of her chair and wrapped his arms round her. 'Thank God. I thought you were going to say no. I was so scared you might have changed your mind about us while I was away.'

A tear trickled down her cheek. 'Ellis, I missed you so much. And I was so scared that you wouldn't want to come back.'

'No. I missed you more with every passing day. And it's never been like that for me before. I couldn't wait to come home.' He stroked her face. 'And now I'm home for good.'

'Ellis, you don't have to give up your old life completely,' she said. 'I don't want you to have any regrets in the future. Maybe if you went out for, I don't know, a couple of weeks every six months, then you could still do the stuff you love and feel that you're making a difference to the world.'

'Though you've taught me that I can make a difference right here—like I did with Helen Perkins and the intra-uterine transfusion,' he said. He paused. 'You're right, I will miss it sometimes—I've spent most of my career working abroad. But what you've suggested could work.'

'But?' She spoke the word that was echoing through his head.

'I'd still hate leaving you behind. I know I asked you before and you said no, but if I was only going out for a really short assignment once in a while, would you consider going with me?'

'If it's only for a really short assignment, then yes, I could cope with that,' she said.

'Good. I love you.' He kissed her. 'And once my clothes are dry, we'll go and tell the world our news.'

She kissed him back. 'That'll be a while yet. So I think maybe we have time to go and have a private celebration, first.'

'That's one of the things I love about you,' he said with a grin. 'You're full of great ideas...'

EPILOGUE

Two years later

ELLIS SAT ON the edge of the bed in the maternity department of the London Victoria, with his arm round Ruby and his finger being clutched very hard by their tiny, red-faced son.

'Life doesn't get any better than this, Mrs Webster,' he said softly. 'And I love you both very, very much.'

'We love you, too,' Ruby said. 'Don't we, Tom?'

In answer, the baby simply yawned, and they both laughed.

'I'm glad you got back in time for his birth,' she said.

'I nearly didn't. First babies are meant to be late, not two weeks early. Especially when their father is working in the middle of nowhere, several hundred miles away, for just one short week, thinking that he probably had a month until the baby arrived.' He rolled his eyes. 'Talk about timing. I think this one's going to be stubborn as anything.'

'Just like his dad,' she teased.

'Getting to the airport, opening my phone and seeing the text from you that you'd gone into labour...I nearly passed out,' he said.

She grinned. 'Tsk. And all the babies you've delivered, Dr Webster.'

'It's very different when it's *your* wife and *your* baby,' he said, and bent to drop a kiss on the baby's forehead. 'Luckily the woman in front of me in the queue for passport control asked me if I was all right—and when I told her my news, she told me to go in front of her. And so did everyone else in the queue, passing it forward. They all made way for me so I didn't have to wait so long to get to you. The kindness of strangers is truly amazing.'

'It certainly is,' she agreed. 'Though you've done your share of giving and kindness, too. Think of it as what goes around, comes around.'

'I guess.' He smiled. 'I love you, Rubes. And our baby. I can hardly believe we made someone so beautiful and so perfect.' He met her gaze. 'How many times have we heard new parents say that and smiled? But it's true. And I can't wait to take you both home.' Home, to the terraced house with a garden they'd bought together just after they'd got married. 'And for all the grandparents to come and see him—because this baby's going to have three sets. Your parents, my parents, and Tom's—because they're practically my parents too and there's no way I'll let them feel left out.'

Ruby smiled at him. 'That's another thing I love about you. You've turned into a real family man.'

'With a little help from you. You've done a lot to thaw my parents out.' He smiled back at her. 'You've changed my life, Ruby. I never thought I could ever be this happy and settled.'

'And I never thought I'd find this kind of happiness

a second time,' she said softly. 'It felt greedy, expecting too much.'

'No—as you said, what goes around, comes around, and you're one of life's givers. If I make you and baby Tom as happy as you both make me—well, that's all I want.' He kissed her. 'I think everyone on the ward is dying to visit you, so I'm going to let them all come and make a fuss of you while I have a shower and get rid of all the travel dust.'

'And the stubble. Looks sexy, but...' She pulled a face. 'Ouch.'

He laughed. 'Yeah. You say that every time. I love you. And Tom. And I'm so proud of you both.'

She laughed back. 'We're proud of you, too. Go and get rid of the travel stuff. And then you can take us home.'

He smiled. 'Your wish, my love, is my command.'

Home.

And he really was home. For good.

* * * * *

MILLS & BOON®
Hardback – July 2015

ROMANCE

MILLS & BOON®
Large Print – July 2015

ROMANCE

The Taming of Xander Sterne	Carole Mortimer
In the Brazilian's Debt	Susan Stephens
At the Count's Bidding	Caitlin Crews
The Sheikh's Sinful Seduction	Dani Collins
The Real Romero	Cathy Williams
His Defiant Desert Queen	Jane Porter
Prince Nadir's Secret Heir	Michelle Conder
The Renegade Billionaire	Rebecca Winters
The Playboy of Rome	Jennifer Faye
Reunited with Her Italian Ex	Lucy Gordon
Her Knight in the Outback	Nikki Logan

HISTORICAL

The Soldier's Dark Secret	Marguerite Kaye
Reunited with the Major	Anne Herries
The Rake to Rescue Her	Julia Justiss
Lord Gawain's Forbidden Mistress	Carol Townend
A Debt Paid in Marriage	Georgie Lee

MEDICAL

How to Find a Man in Five Dates	Tina Beckett
Breaking Her No-Dating Rule	Amalie Berlin
It Happened One Night Shift	Amy Andrews
Tamed by Her Army Doc's Touch	Lucy Ryder
A Child to Bind Them	Lucy Clark
The Baby That Changed Her Life	Louisa Heaton

MILLS & BOON®
Hardback – August 2015

ROMANCE

The Greek Demands His Heir	Lynne Graham
The Sinner's Marriage Redemption	Annie West
His Sicilian Cinderella	Carol Marinelli
Captivated by the Greek	Julia James
The Perfect Cazorla Wife	Michelle Smart
Claimed for His Duty	Tara Pammi
The Marakaios Baby	Kate Hewitt
Billionaire's Ultimate Acquisition	Melanie Milburne
Return of the Italian Tycoon	Jennifer Faye
His Unforgettable Fiancée	Teresa Carpenter
Hired by the Brooding Billionaire	Kandy Shepherd
A Will, a Wish...a Proposal	Jessica Gilmore
Hot Doc from Her Past	Tina Beckett
Surgeons, Rivals...Lovers	Amalie Berlin
Best Friend to Perfect Bride	Jennifer Taylor
Resisting Her Rebel Doc	Joanna Neil
A Baby to Bind Them	Susanne Hampton
Doctor...to Duchess?	Annie O'Neil
Second Chance with the Billionaire	Janice Maynard
Having Her Boss's Baby	Maureen Child

MILLS & BOON®
Large Print – August 2015

ROMANCE

The Billionaire's Bridal Bargain	Lynne Graham
At the Brazilian's Command	Susan Stephens
Carrying the Greek's Heir	Sharon Kendrick
The Sheikh's Princess Bride	Annie West
His Diamond of Convenience	Maisey Yates
Olivero's Outrageous Proposal	Kate Walker
The Italian's Deal for I Do	Jennifer Hayward
The Millionaire and the Maid	Michelle Douglas
Expecting the Earl's Baby	Jessica Gilmore
Best Man for the Bridesmaid	Jennifer Faye
It Started at a Wedding...	Kate Hardy

HISTORICAL

A Ring from a Marquess	Christine Merrill
Bound by Duty	Diane Gaston
From Wallflower to Countess	Janice Preston
Stolen by the Highlander	Terri Brisbin
Enslaved by the Viking	Harper St. George

MEDICAL

A Date with Her Valentine Doc	Melanie Milburne
It Happened in Paris...	Robin Gianna
The Sheikh Doctor's Bride	Meredith Webber
Temptation in Paradise	Joanna Neil
A Baby to Heal Their Hearts	Kate Hardy
The Surgeon's Baby Secret	Amber McKenzie

MILLS & BOON®

Why shop at millsandboon.co.uk?

Each year, thousands of romance readers find their perfect read at millsandboon.co.uk. That's because we're passionate about bringing you the very best romantic fiction. Here are some of the advantages of shopping at www.millsandboon.co.uk:

* **Get new books first**—you'll be able to buy your favourite books one month before they hit the shops

* **Get exclusive discounts**—you'll also be able to buy our specially created monthly collections, with up to 50% off the RRP

* **Find your favourite authors**—latest news, interviews and new releases for all your favourite authors and series on our website, plus ideas for what to try next

* **Join in**—once you've bought your favourite books, don't forget to register with us to rate, review and join in the discussions

Visit **www.millsandboon.co.uk**
for all this and more today!